The Beetles
of
Barraclough
House

*For Mo
in gratitude*

John Evans

by

John Evans

This book is published by
Grosvenor House Publishing Ltd
28 – 30 High Street, Guildford, Surrey, GU1 3HY.
www.grosvenorhousepublishing.co.uk

A CIP record for this book
Is available from the British Library

ISBN 978-1-905529-05-6

To Carys, Gareth and Delyth

CHAPTER ONE

Then, suddenly, there was that noise again.

Henry had heard it before - a sort of metallic clicking sound coming from somewhere behind the wall-boarding in the deeper gloom at the far end of the long, low attic room. It was at a point where the eaves sloped down so that you would have to stoop to avoid banging your head on the sagging ceiling.

Henry stared down from the smeary dormer window at the sulky, dripping shrubbery which bordered the threadbare lawn far, far below. He was filled with self-righteous gloom, his mood exactly fitting the sullen August downpour outside. Every summer, for as long as he could remember, his parents had loaded up the racketing Volvo with tinned food and bottles of cheap wine, and they had set off for two weeks 'holiday' in Uncle Jimmy's crumbling old vicarage deep in the Shropshire countryside.

Oh, there were some good days. When the sun shone, Henry had the run of the unruly acres of the vicarage garden which backed onto the tangled mystery of Trimble's wood on the hillside behind. Henry was an explorer - a leader of men in uncharted wastes. The search for new territories or for hidden treasure was often only halted by the distant tones of the old dinner gong through the gathering dusk. But he was a solitary leader even then, and the triumph of conquest was always lessened by the lack of someone to share with.

Today, Henry was in disgrace. Here he was, banished to his room - and all he'd done was to say 'all right'.

Well actually....

What he'd said was 'all right, all *right*', but it came to the same thing surely? His parents had wanted to spend the afternoon in a boring old church again.

'We're going to Flopton Magna this afternoon, Henry.' his mother had said brightly over lunch. 'There are some really fascinating brasses there, and you're allowed to rub with prior permission of the vicar.'

So then he'd made the mistake of saying that he didn't see the point of rubbing soppy old brasses, and his mother had gone into that I-don't-understand-the-boy-what-have-we-done routine, and Uncle Jimmy had cleared his throat nervously and rushed off to the shelter of his study - and he should have seen the warning signs then, but after a whole afternoon of unusual gravestones in the drizzle yesterday.....

'Why don't you want to do things together as a family?' his mother had asked plaintively - and Henry hadn't **said** anything, but he'd thought **really loudly** about why didn't they play cowboys or lost tribes as a family instead of mouldering around graveyards, and his mum had said 'Well?' very loudly and he'd said:

'All right.'

Well actually:

'All right, *all right.*'

And now he was stuck here for the rest of the day.

Then, suddenly, there was the noise again.

He had noticed it before, but always he had been too busy - about to leave on some expedition into the shrubbery, or called away to another of Uncle Jimmy's disastrous meals. Today, the only distraction was watching the bloated raindrops chasing down the dusty garret window.

In the first long minutes of his captivity, he had toyed with the idea of developing some wasting illness. He would nobly keep the symptoms to himself, bravely hiding his secret pain from his unsuspecting family, until his untimely death shocked his grief-stricken parents into realising what they had done. But it wouldn't work. First, they would think he was sulking, then they'd produce some ghastly medicine which he'd be forced to take about ten times a day; and anyway, being dead would deprive him of the satisfaction of saying he'd told them so.

So now the clicking sound suddenly held an overpowering attraction compared with the alternatives, and cautiously, he made his way towards the source of the noise.

As he approached the gloomy corner of the attic, Henry was blissfully unaware that something really strange was happening. What he did was to walk cautiously on tiptoe for fear of frightening off whatever was making the noise.

What he should have done, as he had in the past, was to crouch down, to double up to avoid bumping his head on the slope of the ceiling, finally ending up on all fours as he approached the wall. What he did this time was to walk - cautiously and soundlessly, with all his thoughts lost in concentration on the rhythmic pattern of clicks. He reached the peeling pinstriped wall, still standing perfectly upright without any feeling that anything peculiar was occurring.

Close up, the pattern of vertical stripes seemed wider and larger than he had remembered it, the fading lines almost an arm's span apart. Henry leant forward and ran his fingers over the roughened surface. It was difficult to see properly, so far from the dust-veiled light of the attic window, but as his fingers brushed over the surface, he felt, with mounting excitement, a regular outline traced under the ancient wallpaper.

It felt just like a secret door.

Carefully, Henry ran his finger nails along the indented oblong, the brittle paper breaking under the pressure to reveal the outline. It certainly looked like a door, but it was a door with no visible handle or hinge, and as Henry stood puzzling over this great discovery, the clicking continued steady and tantalising from behind it. Gently, Henry pushed at the panel, but to no effect at all. The clicking persisted - a regular metallic sound. It was the kind of noise which Henry delighted in making by crushing an empty drinks can and then allowing the tensioned metal to pop in and out under his thumb - the sort of noise which had so often in the past led to a further spell of banishment after a brief lecture on manners over the top of his father's newspaper.

'Click-click!' it invited him, but even when he threw caution to the winds and his entire weight on the mysterious door, it refused to budge an inch.

'Click-click!'

'Damn!' said Henry.

'*Language!*' the voice boomed out so suddenly from behind the panelling that Henry sat down abruptly on the dusty floor-boards. He stayed there for several moments, not sure whether to answer or to run for it. The clicking started up again, as if nothing had happened. Finally Henry's curiosity overcame his fright.

'I'm sorry,' said Henry to the wall. 'I didn't mean to swear - only I know this *is* a door, but I can't work out how to open it.'

'Where were you brought up, laddie?' the booming voice sounded decidedly cross. 'Don't you ever think of asking? Politeness opens door you know - well known saying is that.'

Henry took a deep breath. 'Please may I come in?' he ventured.

'Certainly not,' came the rather unexpected reply, only slightly muffled by the panelling. 'You need to give me the proper password first.'

'But I don't know the password,' Henry protested. He was beginning to get just a little irritated by the performance. 'How can I give you the password if I don't know it?'

'You'll just have to make it up I suppose - that's it, make it up.'

Henry though hard. He'd been to see 'Aladdin' last Christmas. They'd had a password on that. 'How about 'Open Sesame'?' he asked rather doubtfully.

'Funny sort of password that if you ask me - still, you could try it I suppose. Couldn't do any harm.'

Henry cleared his throat. 'Open Sesame!' he shouted.

And suddenly there wasn't a door there at all any more, but just a square opening in the wall- and standing in the opening was

A gigantic Black Beetle.

Henry stared. The beetle towered over him as it stood squarely in the opening, shuffling from foot to foot to foot. It was dressed, as Henry might have expected in a shining black tail coat, of the sort his father had worn to his wedding, but rather unexpectedly, it seemed also to be wearing an extremely tall top hat, which added at least another foot to its already impressive height. One pair of arms was tucked under the shining coat tails of its wing cases, while with another pair it was scratchig thoughtfully behind the long antennae which sprouted, quivering out of the sides of the hat.

The beetle glared at Henry. It was clearly a beetle which was not amused.

'No need to shout.' it said sternly.

CHAPTER TWO

For several dozen clicks Henry could do nothing but stare at the sight before him. He had seen beetles before often enough - once he had even kept quite a sizeable specimen in a matchbox, until his mother had found it one day when she was trying to light the gas stove. But this was a beetle to end all beetles, and his heart was filled with a wild excitement at the prospect of actually being able to talk to the creature. Here was a story for old Beamish, his biology teacher, who had poured scorn on his claim to have a four foot earthworm

'Try sticking a pin in that one,' he thought to himself, as he conjured up a quick daydream in which he produced the angry beetle out of a hamper on Beamish's desk.

He was brought out of his dream abruptly by a positive barrage of clicks. The beetle was becoming impatient.

'Shut your mouth, boy. Don't you know it's rude to stare at people? Anyway, we're going to be late if we don't get a move on.' With that the beetle leaned forward imposingly and, tugging at the gold chain, produced a pocket watch the size of a small turnip which it swung to and fro in front of Henry's eyes as though trying to hypnotise him.

'Late for what?' Henry had the distinct feeling that events were getting ahead of his understanding.

'The meeting of course,' the beetle gave Henry a pitying look. It had clearly formed a low opinion of Henry's intelligence. It restored the watch to the pocket on the bulge of its waistcoat and swung smartly on its heel. It was a move which lost much of its military precision, not to mention its dignity by the need to tuck two of its legs out at right angles to avoid tangling them with the other two.

Then it set off in a kind of rolling waddle down the narrow passageway which led downwards at a sharp slope into the uninhabited depths of Barraclough House.

Henry followed the broad, swaying shoulders which seemed to fill the corridor ahead of him. Looking to left and right at the cobwebbed walls, he saw that here he was among the bones, the skeleton of Barraclough House. No-one, he was sure (no human, that is) could have trodden this forgotten corridor since the days when the house was first built a hundred years or more ago.

The passage wound and twisted, and Henry resolutely followed the faint glimmer of light reflected from the shiny back of the beetle. Suddenly his guide halted and beckoned him forward. Henry found himself looking over the edge of a sheer cliff, which disappeared in darkness some unfathomable distance below.

'Bit of a problem laddie,' said the beetle. It stood there with its arms tucked under its coat tails, and lifted its hat to scratch thoughtfully between its feelers. 'Tell you the truth, I usually have to fly the next bit - though I'm not as young as I used to be, you know.' it added confidingly.

'Oh,' said Henry. There didn't seem to be much else he could say.

'Don't suppose you're much of a hand at this flying thing?'

Henry looked over into the gulf, and tried flapping his arms a bit by way of experiment.

'No,' he admitted sadly. 'I'm not really up on it at all.'

'Well, I'll just wait for you on the other side,' the beetle continued cheerfully. 'It's not very far.' and with that it parted its coat tails to reveal an enormous expanse of surprisingly gossamer wings which it unfurled elaborately, like an old gentleman putting up an umbrella.

'Wait!' Henry called, but it was too late. The beetle had taken several preparatory wheezes, and then closed its eyes and jumped. At first it seemed to just fall, and Henry thought it would disappear for ever into the chasm, but then, with a deafening whirring and wheezing, it was off into the shadows beyond the gulf, leaving Henry alone and forlorn on the brink.

Henry looked despairingly around him. There was no sign of a bridge or any other means of crossing the gap. This, he supposed, was the end of the adventure, so soon after it had begun. He would just have to make his way back to the boredom of the attic. Somehow, the thought of that dismal rain-bounded room spurred him on, and he began to examine his surroundings more closely in the dim light of the tunnel.

Clearly the thought of climbing down was out of the question, and there seemed little point in trying anyway, since the gulf in front of him looked quite bottomless. Henry turned his attention to the walls, and with mounting excitement, realised that there was at least a real possibility of a way forward.

The walls were constructed of a series of regular, rectangular blocks which might have been bricks were it not for the sheer size of them. In between them, the mortar on which they were laid had been carelessly slapped, and had somehow worn away over the years to leave deep, parallel runnels which ran outwards and away from him across the canyon. Henry found that with his toes jammed firmly into the lower course, he could just work his fingers into the one above and hang, spider like on the face of the wall.

Gingerly, he began edging his way into the gloom. His face was crammed up against the damp, rough surface of the wall, and he felt his heart beat faster as he edged slowly onwards.

Shuffle the left foot sideways, force the toe of his shoe into the crack, then cautiously release his hold with the right hand to ease it outwards and curl his fingers over the edge of the crack above. Now transfer the weight onto his right foot and slowly bring the left hand, then the foot, up to the right. Now begin the whole painful business again.

After some five minutes of hard labour, he was beginning to feel very tired indeed. The wall seemed never-ending, and he moved so slowly that the beetle would surely be long gone if he did ever reach the safety of the other side. Fighting back a rising panic, which threatened to glue him there for ever, he forced himself to move more quickly, building up a rhythm, and scuttling like a crab across the face of the wall.

The disaster struck.

As he transferred his weight for the hundredth time onto his right foot, the crumbling mortar suddenly gave way. For a long moment, he clung to the face of the wall, his fingers scrabbling desperately for grip. Then he was falling helplessly into the void.

Henry closed his eyes tightly as the wind rushed past him. He gritted his teeth, waiting for the crash which would be followed by blackness.

With a jerk, he stopped falling. It was as if a parachute had opened above him; and then he was gently rising again, and moving forward steadily as he rose. As his shocked senses returned to him, he was aware of a downward breeze on his face, and of a mechanical whirring noise above him which was punctuated by loud wheezing sounds.

Then as he dared to open his eyes again, he was gently deposited back on firm ground, and he saw a very out of breath beetle fussily folding back its wings under their shiny cases. The beetle gave a last tuck to the wings and turned to look sternly at the boy.

'See what you mean about flying,' it said. 'Worst exhibition I ever saw. I've seen ants fly better than that.'

'That wasn't flying,' Henry explained. 'That was - well falling actually. Thank goodness you came back when you did.' he added gratefully.

'Couldn't wait all day laddie,' the beetle said reproachfully. 'Got to get on - the meeting you know.' it added mysteriously. It began waddling off again, away from the cliff edge down the continuing corridor. Then it stopped suddenly and turned to look at the boy closely.

'About this falling thing,' it said slowly.

'What about it?'

'I should give that up if I were you laddie,' advised the beetle. 'No future in it - no future at all.'

CHAPTER THREE

After what seemed like several hours of fumbling, ever downwards through the gloomy tunnel they quite suddenly reached a solid, studded door, set into the wall at a point where the passage made an abrupt turn to the right. The beetle stopped, and began hammering away at an iron knocker set in the door's centre.

'Deaf as a post, deaf as a post,' it muttered, clicking furiously. Henry waited patiently a few paces back in the shadows. After a further furious battering, the door finally swung inwards, and a stream of brilliant light flooded in on them, leaving Henry blinking helplessly.

'Bout time too, Dumble,' he heard the beetle say, as he struggled to regain his sight. 'Been knocking for the best part of a minute. Some watchman you are, I must say.'

'N-n-n-ot my fault,' the reply was a high pitched stammer. 'Y-y-y-uo're late. We were going to start without you.'

' I like that, young Dumble. And me with a guest too,' the beetle waved a couple of arms in the direction of the blinking figure behind it. 'Not just any guest mind,' it added grandly. 'It's the one we've been waiting for all these years.'

Triumphantly, he stepped back and propelled Henry ahead of him into the bright sunlight beyond the door. On the threshold, Henry tripped over some unseen obstacle and promptly measured his length on the moss outside.

'He does that,' explained the beetle. 'Falling, he calls it. He did a really big one back there at the big gap, but I think I interrupted him.' he leaned forward to his companion and continued in a loud, confidential whisper. 'He doesn't fly, you know - not so much as a flap.'

Sitting on the damp moss, Henry was at last able to examine the newcomer. It was another beetle, not quite as tall as the first, but almost completely round. As he stood looking down at Henry, two pairs of arms were busily scratching all over the protruding globe of its belly. Then one pair switched abruptly to scrabble away under its wing cases. From somewhere, Henry caught a strong whiff of farmyard manure.

'Allow me to introduce you,' said the first beetle. 'Boy - this is the Dumble Dor, also known in common speech as the Lousy Watchman - he's a dung beetle, you know,' he added, noticing Henry's wrinkled nose.

'pleased to meet you,' said Henry, rather doubtfully. Nothing in his upbringing had ever prepared him properly for polite greeting of beetles and he was wondering whether he should shake hands, and if so, which one.

'I myself, by the way,' continued the first beetle, 'am Xestobium Rufovillosum, more commonly perhaps known as the Watch Beetle. I am in charge of the house,' he finished importantly.

Henry now had time to look around him. He was in a mossy-floored clearing in the old shrubbery which sidled up to the gable end of Barraclough House. Behind him, the house itself rose up sheer to an unimaginable height, but he gave it no more than a cursory glance, because his attention was drawn to the far side of the clearing by the strangest gathering of creatures he had ever seen.

An improvised table had been made from a rotten tree branch, running the entire length of the clearing. On each side of the table was seated a row of assorted beetles in colours which ranged from sombre black to brilliant iridescent green. One or two of them even had enormous antlers on the tops of their heads. What they all had in common was that they were all staring in stunned silence at Henry.

16

As far as Henry could see there were only two vacant places. At the foot of the table was a roughly made chair, but at the head was a sight which made Henry gasp.

This was no common chair, but the most wonderful throne, its arms and back gilded and gleaming in the leaf-filtered light of the clearing. The legs, arms and back of the throne were studded with what appeared to be precious gems which sparkled suddenly as a shaft of sunlight broke through the leaf canopy above. The seat was of some beautiful satin cloth, interwoven with threads of silver and gold.

Solemnly, the Watch beetle led the wondering boy to the throne, and with a sweeping bow, invited him to sit. Then he lumbered off down the silent table to take his place at the foot. For a long moment, the assembly of beetles stared at the boy. Henry stared back, open-mouthed. Then the Watch Beetle spoke.

'Gentlemen, he has come to us,' he said solemnly. 'At last the long wait is over. The empty throne is filled. Our troubles are ended.'

With that all the beetles suddenly let out a resounding cheer, and began a deafening pounding on the table top with as many arms as they could find room to hammer. Then, just as suddenly, the noise stopped, as the Watch Beetle spread his arms wide. Once again there was an equally deafening silence.

'Silence!' said the Watch Beetle, loudly and unnecessarily. 'The boy will speak'

Henry stared round at the two rows of expectant beetle faces before him. He wondered whether he should stand up, but quickly decided that his trembling knees wouldn't hold him. Nothing that had happened so far had prepared him for this. What on earth was he going to say?

He cleared his throat nervously.

'It's very nice of you to invite me,' he said weakly.

And once again, the thunderous applause rang across the clearing.

CHAPTER FOUR

As suddenly as it had begun, the tumultuous applause ended, and then, as if by some secret signal, all the beetles leapt up and began beetling off in all directions into the undergrowth. Soon the only ones left were Henry, the Watch Beetle and one other - a Handsome, slim beetle, cloaked from head to foot in brilliant red.

'He doesn't look much like his portrait,' the beetle said doubtfully.

Solemnly, the Watch Beetle introduced them.

'Boy, this is the Cardinal Beetle - officially Pyrochroa Serraticornis. He'll be looking after you from now on. I myself have to stay with the house.' he explained proudly.

'but where am I going?' Henry was beginning to feel more than a little anxious. 'I'll be late for tea.....'

'Nonsense boy,' the Watch Beetle was scornful. 'There's no tea-time any more - not until you've finished the job you came for. The Cardinal here will take you to the Palace - and tonight it's the grand ball. The whole of beetledom will be there to honour your arrival.'

'But what am I supposed to be doing here?'

'Patience boy - Rome wasn't built in a day you know. You go along with the Cardinal here and you'll soon get the hang of things.' He leaned forward confidingly. 'I should just cut down on the falling thing though, if I were you - doesn't impress them at all you know.' and with that he was gone, back into the dusty tunnels of the ancient house. Henry turned to the Cardinal.

'Well, your Holiness,' he said. 'Where do we have to go now?'

The beetle's reaction was a complete surprise to Henry. For a moment it just stared at him, then it let out a high-pitched squeal of laughter. Within moments it was rolling on the moss at his feet clutching its sides and wriggling its legs in an ecstasy of mirth.

'Hee, hee, hee,' it gasped. 'I like that one. Your 'oliness indeed. Juss wait till I tell the missus and the grubs about that one - your 'oliness. Fit to die. Hee, hee, hee.'
'I'm sorry,' Henry stammered. 'Assumed.'

'Assumed is it? Well I never did. I'm the Cardinal see, 'cause of these red togs I always wear. I s'pose you'll be calling the Ladybirds 'melady' next,' and he went off into further peals of mirth at the idea. Henry waited patiently for him to calm down,

Eventually, the giggles subsided, and the Cardinal had recovered enough composure to dust himself down, though his antennae still quivered alarmingly.

'Right then - we'd better be off,' it said briskly, and set off at breakneck speed into the shrubbery. Henry followed nervously, trying to set aside all thoughts of his missed tea, although to tell the truth he was beginning to feel very hungry indeed.

He wondered vaguely if they had missed him yet at home, but then remembered that Uncle Jimmy was getting tea today, to allow his parents the longest possible stay at Flopton Magna. Without a reminder, Uncle Jimmy would sometimes go for days on end without thinking of food, so his absence should remain undiscovered, at least for the time being. Very soon, in any case, all thought of home was lost in contemplation of his surroundings.

They must, he thought, be in a part of the garden that had been off limits to him, because certainly nothing in his past experience held any resemblance to what his wondering gaze took in. The undergrowth on either side of the narrow path which they were following had all the luxuriance and denseness of a tropical rainforest. In many places, the path was completely overhung by vegetation, so that for some distance, they would be plunged into a deep green twilight, full of mysterious rustling and scuffling, just beyond the range of his vision.

The most astonishing thing, however, was the trees. He had been to Kew Gardens once, when his parents were going through a botanical phase, and there he had stared in amazement at the giant Redwoods, which soared seemingly above the clouds, their ridged and scaly trunks so wide of girth that to run round them was to arrive breathless back at the starting point. The trees which now bordered the path were of a size which put the Redwoods to shame, and looking up at the distant canopy, high above, left him dizzy and scared. He would have liked to slow his pace and take in the wonder of this strange, gigantic world, but the Cardinal hurried on relentlessly, its feathered feet scuffling through the leaf mould in its haste.

They had been walking for what seemed like hours now, and Henry's legs were becoming decidedly tired. Strange, he thought, how far the grounds of Barraclough House extended beyond his wildest imaginings when he had played his lonely games on the margin of the threadbare lawns. They were just rounding a bend in the path, when they were confronted by a plump beetle in shining green.

It was standing in the middle of the path, frantically waving both pairs of arms like a windmill in a gale. Since it was in any case quite impossible to get round its flailing bulk, the Cardinal drew to a halt, and the newcomer waddled to meet them.

'Cat!' it hissed urgently, 'Cat!'

And without further ado, Henry found himself being bundled into a pile of rotting vegetation at the edge of the track. As he lay there, spitting bits of leaf from the corner of his mouth, he was aware of a thunderous crashing through the undergrowth growing steadily nearer.

His heart in his mouth, Henry burrowed into the leaf mould and covered his head with his hands. They lay there hardly breathing, while the crashing grew to a crescendo, then just as suddenly, began to die away into the depths of the wood. When all had been silent for several minutes, the Cardinal cautiously raised its head above the surface of the leaves.

'You can come out now,' it announced, as Henry struggled into the light and air, and sat picking bits of undergrowth out of his jumper. The green beetle had already vanished up the path. Henry turned to the Cardinal, who was busy preening his wing cases.

'Did he really say 'cat'?' he asked.

'Tricky fellers yer cats,' was the matter-of-fact reply. 'They don't generally mean much harm - only playful as you might say, but it don't feel too playful if they up and jump on you out of some bush. I 'ad a cousin got jumped on once - flat as a pancake.' he finished with rather more relish than was strictly necessary. The he turned and scuttled off up the path again.

'Must get on -must get on,' he called over his shoulder, and Henry, with a hundred unanswered questions about cats pounding in his head, trudged wearily in his wake.

Twilight was falling by the time they reached their destination, and Henry was by now distinctly ravenous. It was easy to see they had reached journey's end, because there in front of them at last was the palace.

They had arrived at a large clearing in the centre of which stood the biggest oak tree Henry had ever seen. It was an oak which had at some time been riven by lightening, so that its upper part, high above the floor of the clearing, was blackened and withered. At its base, in the tangled buttresses of its massive roots, there was a sort of opening or archway.

The archway was flanked by two enormous and brightly painted garden gnomes.

Proudly, the Cardinal led him up to this imposing entrance, and stood aside for him to lead the way through into the interior of the tree. Henry had to stoop slightly to get through the arch but, once inside, the vast hollow of the trunk reached skywards, like a gigantic chimney, to a tiny circle of fading daylight far, far above.

And a chimney indeed it was, because right in the middle of the roughly circular floor, a fire was blazing brightly, and in its dancing light, Henry saw to his astonishment, that the room was actually furnished.

CHAPTER FIVE

In the light of the fire, and under the flickering gleam of two large, branched candlesticks, a long table had been laid with shining silverware, laden with the most spectacular feast that Henry could have imagined.

There were bowls of fruit and exotic looking berries in brilliant splashes of red and green. There were strange fungi whose subtle shades varied from pale creamy-white to deep regal purple. There were nuts and chestnuts, their polished shells shining in the candle light. There were salads made from leaves from delicate, translucent green to deep russet. There were bowls filled to overflowing with herbs and roots, such as Henry had never seen - mysterious shapes and colours, arranged in great swirling patterns on the creaking table top.

Henry stared in awe at the feast before him - a feast fit for a king. It is hard to say how long he would have stood there, if the Cardinal hadn't given him a gentle nudge forward into the room. Rushing past him, it pointed importantly to a chair set at the head of the table. It was a chair similar to the throne on which he had earlier sat to make his unpromising first speech to the assembled beetles, except that this one was plainer, lacking the gilt and jewels of the throne.

Henry sat down, and as though by magic, he was suddenly surrounded by black shiny-coated beetles, which had appeared out of the dimness of some recess in the tree-room to wait on him. With carefully rehearsed movements, they proceeded to pile Henry's plate with all that was most choice amongst the spread of food before him. Eagerly, Henry began to sample the strange assortment on his plate.

As he tried each of the different items on his plate, Henry found that the taste was as varied as the display had been colourful. There were bright, crinkled berries which began as a bitterness on the tip of the tongue, but which burst surprisingly into sweetness as he bit through the tough skins. There were mushrooms which tasted of the forest floor itself, damp and musty. There were herbs which sparkled like sherbet on the roof of his mouth. There were nuts which hinted at the smoke of woodfires. There were tastes which he had never before experienced, and which he was at a loss to describe - tastes which left him with a strange longing as he swallowed, at the thought that he would never again experience them for the first time.

And all the time, in a solemn, silent ritual, the waiter beetles wove a dance around him as they refilled his plate with even more and stranger foods.

Finally Henry felt that he could eat no more. 'Thank you,' he said pushing his plate aside. 'That was wonderful. But I honestly couldn't eat another thing.'

The waiter beetles melted away into the shadows and the Cardinal beetle appeared at his side. From a crystal decanter, he poured into Henry's silver cup, a clear, golden liquid. Henry raised the cup to his lips and sipped.

The liquid rolled smoothly over his tongue, releasing a glorious taste which was the nectar of a thousand summer flowers, all interwoven, yet somehow each one distinct. The liquid was still, yet it sparkled, cool yet it warmed the throat, leaving a sleepy afterglow of well-being. Henry sipped again. He closed his eyes, and felt as though he were gazing over a midsummer meadow, its buttercups, clover, cowslips dancing before him in a warm breeze. He tasted the strident yellow of toads flax, the gentle lilac of Lady's Smock, and the icy chill of Harebell. He rolled the liquid languidly around his mouth. The taste was somehow never constant. There would be a sudden explosion of red poppies, a bitter tang of thistles, and somewhere in the haunting background of the aftertaste, a hint of rare orchids, hiding shyly but invitingly, just beyond the reach of his taste.

Henry realised with regret that the cup was empty. The Cardinal had disappeared for the moment, and he was at last able to take in his surroundings, sitting in a warm glow of contentment at the head of the long table.

The room, as he might have expected, was circular, its walls leaning inwards as they rose towards the ever-darkening patch of sky far above. Only half the room was visible from his place at the table, the other half being hidden behind a long, folding screen. The screen was made up of a series of panels, and for some time Henry gazed at this, trying to work out the meaning of the delicate pattern of the material, until he realised with a start that it was covered entirely with the wings of butterflies, arranged in symmetrical patterns which glowed in the light of the fire. The other furniture in the room was all of the same elaborately carved type as the chair on which he was sitting - tall shining black cupboards threw distorted shadows onto the walls, while mysterious wooden chests, bound in strips of brightly shining metal stood a little back from the chattering fire.

Further examination of the room was prevented for Henry however by the strange behaviour of the butterfly-wing screen. His attention was first caught by a furtive rustling coming from that part of the room. As he watched, fascinated, the screen began to fold itself up[and walk away, and he realised that what he had been looking at was a screen composed entirely of living butterflies. Now before his eyes, the butterflies were disentangling themselves, folding their wings and forming into a precise line two abreast. As the last section of the screen transformed itself, the line set off at a brisk march for the door.

The last butterfly to unfold, a handsome red Admiral, approached Henry importantly.

'Our card, sir,' it said grandly, producing from somewhere a small square of pasteboard. 'Please don't hesitate to get in touch. You will find our rates most reasonable.' and it turned and marched smartly off after its retreating companions.

Henry looked at the card. It was an impressive looking business card, with a telephone number printed in gold lettering along the top. In each corner, there was a drawing of a butterfly, its wings extended, and in the middle, in heavy black were the words:


```
        LIFESCREENS Ltd
   ADD A SPLASH OF COLOUR
      TO ANY FUNCTION
```


Henry tucked the card into the pocket of his trousers, and began once again to take an interest in his surroundings.

The far end of the room, revealed by the departure of the screen, was dominated by a four-poster bed, its silken canopy shining in the firelight. The Cardinal was waiting patiently beside the bed, and as |Henry got up from his chair and crossed the room, he drew back the silken curtains to reveal a princely costume spread out on the embroidered counterpane.

'Are these for me?' asked Henry, bewildered.

'Got to look your best for the ball,' the Cardinal said urgently, and Henry, discarding his own rough clothes, put on the delicate silken garments, and buttoned up the jewel encrusted waistcoat. Finally he clipped the short velvet cloak about his neck, and stood before the full-length mirror beside the bed, every inch the Prince.

'That's more like it,' said the Cardinal, bundling Henry's clothes into a chest. 'And now, it's time for the ball.'

CHAPTER SIX

Henry became aware of the faint strains of merry music from outside the palace, as he followed the Cardinal to the door. He stepped out into a clearing transformed.

It had now grown completely dark, but in the woodland glade, all was light and merriment. The glade was illuminated by scores of glow worms which hung from the lowest branches of the trees at the margin of the clearing. At intervals across the floor of the glade, stout posts had been erected, and each one was topped by a brightly glowing insect, their shining tails pulsating in time to the music.

The lifescreens team were back in action, forming the backdrop to an orchestra of crickets and grasshoppers who were busily sawing out a brisk dance tune. At the far end of the clearing was a raised platform, on which were seated the most important apparently, of the beetles, and at their centre was the empty throne.

The Cardinal solemnly threaded his way through the crowd of dancing beetles on the floor of the clearing, and handed Henry to the throne. As soon as he was seated, a waiter beetle appeared at his elbow with a cup of the golden liquid which had delighted him earlier.

And so the evening passes in a confusion of song and dancing and bright conversation, until suddenly it was late into the night, and the imposing Stag Beetle to Henry's left was nodding in his chair.

Henry was suddenly aware of that same dunghill smell which had assailed him at the entrance to the house earlier. He turned to find the Dumble Dor had sidled up to the throne.

'Psst!' said the Dor theatrically - and unnecessarily.

'Hello, Mr. Dumble,' Henry was intrigued. The fat beetle had the look of a conspirator about him.

'Word to the wise - word to the wise,' hissed the beetle glancing furtively at the nodding Stag Beetle on Henry's left.

'What is it Mr. Dumble?' asked Henry puzzled.

'Look at them,' whispered the Dor disgustedly. 'Not a care in the world as you might say. And with all that hanging over them, you'd think they'd have better things to do than dance the night away. They'll pay for it - you mark my words.'

'So what exactly is the problem?' asked Henry.

'Don't have nothing to do with ants - not if they asks you. Never can trust an ant.'

The Cardinal appeared at Henry's side. The Dor cast him an anxious glance, then waddled hurriedly off across the emptying dance floor.

'What was all that about ants?' asked Henry.

The Cardinal coughed. 'Don't you worry your head about that sire. It's time you were off to bed. we've got an early meeting of the Council tomorrow.'

Once again Henry threaded his way through the revellers, fewer in number now, but clearly intent on extracting the last drop of enjoyment out of this once in a lifetime festivity.

As Henry snuggled down between silken sheets, he had just time to wonder what would be happening at Barraclough House. Were they looking for him? Had they called the police? But somehow it was so far away and in such a different world, that he felt incapable of worrying about it, and moments later, blissful sleep overcame him.

CHAPTER SEVEN

Henry awoke with a start. For a moment he was filled with panic at the strangeness of his surroundings, then he remembered with relief, the events of yesterday and sat up in bed, eager to explore once again, this magical world which lay so unsuspected in the shrubbery of Barraclough House.

The massive door to his palace had been flung wide, and the sunlight flooded in, full of the music of birdsong. Henry felt excitement stirring in him. This was a day for real adventures - and what a world this was in which to have them.

Moments later, the Cardinal appeared at his bedside, carrying a large, finely decorated cup on a silver tray. Silently it handed the tray to Henry, and then began laying out a suit of clothing on the bed from one of the steel-bound trunks. Henry watched curiously.

These were no silken robes, but a sort of battledress, all greens and browns to camuflage the wearer against the woodland undergrowth.

Henry sipped the liquid cautiously. It was a strange infusion of herbs, bittersweet and tangy to the taste, and as he sipped he was conscious that the slight feeling of hunger which had hovered in the background at his awakening was now entirely gone. He felt refreshed and ready for whatever the day might bring.

The Cardinal was, as always, filled with urgency and self-importance.

'We must hurry,' it said, indicating the clothes. 'The Council meeting is due to start soon, and it can hardly begin without you, now can it?'
Henry put on the clothes. The cloth felt rough and scratchy against

his skin, but his appearance in the mirror sent a thrill of pride through him. He was a real soldier - more than that, he was a general, who would stand at the head of his troops and lead them into triumphant battle against an unjust enemy. As if to complete the image, the Cardinal burrowed in yet another chest and produced a long, dress sword in a jewel-studded scabbard, which it held out to the boy.

strapped it to his side, then gingerly drew the finely etched steel blade from its sheath, and gazed at the strange characters inscribed on the gleaming page.

'Come on,' the Cardinal interrupted his daydream, and they set off through the door into the sparkling morning, Henry hastily returning the sword to his side as he followed. There would be time later he hoped, to examine that strange writing more closely, but for now it was all he could do to keep from falling over the sword as it swung at his side in his hurried pursuit of the scuttling beetle.

They set off this time in a different direction from the path which had brought them on the previous day. Stealing a glance over his shoulder as they left the clearing, Henry felt a tug of disappointment to see only an old oak tree, blasted by lightening at the centre of the glade. All signs of the majesty and of the festivities of the previous night had vanished with the dew of this magnificent morning.

The Cardinal was leading him into an area of denser undergrowth, where the shrubbery overhung the path, leaving them once again in the dim, green undersea light which he remembered from yesterday's journey. Finally they reached a tall overhanging bank, festooned with ivy, which hung downwards towards the woodland floor. This was obviously their destination, and the full Council was there to greet them.

The Cardinal stood respectfully aside, and Henry ducked under the overhanging ivy to take his now accustomed place at the head of the table. He tried to do so with dignity becoming his apparent rank, but unfortunately, his sword seemed to have a life of its own, and his first attempt ended with the scabbard hooked around the table leg and himself in an untidy heap on the floor.

Henry blushed furiously as he picked himself up, but the assembly of beetles simply waited politely for him to untangle himself. It was as though they had determined to allow him one more indulgence in his favourite but bizarre pastime, before beginning the serious business of the day. Final Henry was seated, his sword safely tucked to one side.

At the opposite end of the table sat the giant Stag Beetle of the night before, and he was obviously a personage of some importance in this gathering, because as soon as the commotion died down at Henry's end of the table, he rose ponderously to his feet and tapped loudly, as though to deepen further the expectant hush of the assembled beetles.

The Stag Beetle cleared its throat. They waited.

The Stag Beetle began fumbling about in the folds of his wing cases. He produced a pair of half-moon glasses which he dusted fussily, before balancing them improbably between his antlers. One of the smaller beetles shuffled nervously. The Stag Beetle glared him into silence through the glinting lenses of the glasses.

There was a large leather bound book on the table in front of the Stag Beetle. He opened the heavy cover, and leaning with hands spread on either side of the opened volume, he stared at the other beetles over the tops of his glasses.

'This,' he said finally. 'is an historic moment for us all - historic.' he paused dramatically. Henry found he had an irresisitible urge to fidget under the steely gaze.
'At last,' he continued, after the pause had lengthened unbearably, 'At last One has come as predicted in the Book of the Scarab, to lead us. He has come as written, out of the Big House, and the Watch

Beetle's long wait has finally been crowned with success.'

At this point several of the more enthusiastic beetles broke into spontaneous applause, only to be hushed again by loud throat-clearings on the part of the Stag Beetle.

'I shall read to you,' he continued, 'from chapter ninety-three of the Book of the Scarab.' again there was much clearing of the throat as he flicked through the pages.

'Ah yes - here!' and his voice took on the echoing note of the kind that Henry had heard the vicar use for his Sunday sermon. 'There will come finally one who is NOT OF OUR KIND to lead you. His courage will be beyond measure, and his nobility will shine as a light in our darkness.'

The Stag Beetle paused, and with a sweeping gesture, indicated the nervous figure of Henry at the head of the table.

'One NOT OF OUR KIND,' he repeated dramatically, his arm outstretched towards Henry. All the other beetles turned their combined gaze on poor Henry, who was beginning to wish the floor would open up under him. Hesitantly he got to his feet. All this talk about being courageous was beginning to make him very nervous indeed. The beetles waited, ready to hang on his every word.

Henry cleared his throat.

'Perhaps you could tell me what exactly you want me to do?' he said.

And for the second time in two short days, the woodlands rang to a tumult of applause.

CHAPTER EIGHT

'But you all seem so happy,' Henry protested. 'I mean - there was the ball last night and everything. I can't believe that you need someone like me to save you. I mean - what do you need saving from?'

'Ah - I wish it were so,' the Stag Beetle answered dolefully. 'It's a long story, and will need patience in the telling. But you must know how sorry we now are compared with the happy world we once knew.' and he began to tell Henry the story of the beetles' retreat to exile from the warmth of their former kingdom, to what he described as the 'broken remnants' of their present world.

There were just eight of them present now in what the Stag Beetle had grandly described as the Council of the Scarab. The rest of the company had long since departed, apparently happy to leave matters in the hands of this select group.

Seated at the table besides Henry, the Stag Beetle and the Cardinal, were a weevil with a strange elongated nose, a bright green beetle with shiny, oily wing-cases, the Dumble Dor (who sat apart from the rest of the company) and two smaller stag beetles, with less important horns, who showed an annoying tendency to nudge each other and fidget.

The Stag Beetle had begun with solemn introductions, reeling off a string of impressive Latin-sounding names.

'This is Curiculo Nucum,' he began indicating the weevil, who gave a rather haughty twitch of its nose in reply. 'He represents our weevil brethren.'

'Next' - turning to the green beetle. 'Lytta Vesicatoria - from the family of oil beetles. The Dumble Dor and the Cardinal you have already met, I believe.' He paused to give the Dumble Dor a hard stare, while at the same time applying to his proboscis, a small square of lace handkerchief which he had extracted with great delicacy from his waistcoat pocket. The Dumble Dor smiled broadly back, sitting tilted back comfortably in his chair, and scratching absent-mindedly at his shiny paunch.

'Finally, my two colleagues Dorcu Parallelipedus - They are *lesser* Stag Beetles - here to take the minutes.' he glared emphatically at the fidgeting pair.

There then followed a noisy argument about over representation of the Stag Beetle fraternity, which might have gone on for some time if Henry hadn't interrupted. Since the meeting had begun he had felt a growing sense of annoyance at the way he was being expected to sit and listen. Now he came to think about it, he hadn't had any say in the proceedings since he'd first met the Watch Beetle yesterday afternoon. If he was such an important person, he thought, then they had a funny way of showing it.

'Excuse me,' he said, and instantly there was a deathly hush. 'But would someone please tell me exactly what I'm doing here?'

The Stag Beetle stared open-mouthed in astonishment. 'But you're our leader of course,' he said 'I thought that was obvious to one and all.'

'Funny sort of leader if you ask me,' said Henry warming to his subject. 'Since I got here, nobody's asked me what I think about anything, or if I'd like this or that or what I'd like to do. I don't even get a say in what I wear or where I go.'

'But - we thought...' the Stag Beetle was taken aback.

'You didn't think,' Henry broke in. 'You didn't think of me at all - only your grand rotten plan whatever that is - if there **is** a plan that is 'cause I've heard precious little so far about one. Now - if I'm a leader, it strikes me it's about time you lot started letting me lead.'

There was a stunned silence. The Stag Beetle sat vigorously polishing his glasses. Even the two lesser Stags were shocked into momentary stillness. The silence was suddenly broken by the sound of solitary applause.

'Well done, lad,' the Dumble Dor was grinning wider than ever. 'That's telling him. I knew I should like you as soon as I saw you - what with that falling thing you do and everything. And you haven't sniffed at me once!' he finished as if that decided everything.

'Now', said Henry. 'I think you'd better start with your names. I can't cope with those Latin ones you just gave me, so I'll just call you Oily' - he pointed to the green beetle. 'And you two can be Dorc One and Dorc Two - though how I shall ever tell you apart, I don't know.' meekly the beetles accepted this impromptu re-christening.

'Now,' Henry continued purposefully. 'Let's get back to the question I keep asking -what am I here for, and please,' he held up his hand. 'No applause this time. Just tell me.'

'Well - to save us all of course,' said the Stag Beetle as though he was stating the blindingly obvious. 'You've come to save us, just the way it says you will in the Book of the Scarab - chapter ninety-three.'

And that's when Henry made his remark about how happy they all seemed, and how there didn't seem to be anything to save them from. And the Stag Beetle had droned on, reading great chunks out of the leather-bound book, and he was finally beginning to wish he hadn't asked.

The story was full of long boring passages about their flight from freedom in the Dark Days - full of long words of the sort Uncle Jimmy used when he forgot himself. The Stag Beetle still droned on and on , and it was like one of those history lessons where you suddenly remember that you think you forgot to feed your hamster this morning, and by the time you've decided that that was probably yesterday morning, and that you particularly remember giving him a sunflower seed to peel when you put the bowl in his cage, you've missed a big chunk, and you can't make much sense of the rest, so you concentrate on retying your shoelace without the teacher noticing, and then she always says, 'Well Henry - is it?' and you say 'Yes -well no,' and everybody laughs....

Eventually the Stag Beetle came to a halt and solemnly closed the big book.

'That was interesting,' said Henry lying bravely. 'But I'm not sure I follow all of it.' He turned to the Dumble Dor who was picking his mandibles with a bit of straw.

'Perhaps you could give me your version of the story - just to clear up one or two minor points,' he added vaguely - he'd heard his headmaster use that phrase at a parents' evening, and he was glad now he'd saved it for just such an occasion as this.

'Well my boy, it was like this,' the Dumble Dor scratched thoughtfully under his armpit for a moment. 'It was the ants see - they kicked us out.'

The silence which followed was broken by a loud belch from the Dumble Dor.

'Now how about a spot of lunch?' he asked cheerfully.

CHAPTER NINE

Henry settled back happily against the mossy bank in the warmth of the afternoon sun. Lunch had held all the same excitement of the meal of the night before, and now he felt full and contented, just soaking up the sunshine. The last hours had been so full of activity and bustle that he was grateful now to have a moment or two with nothing to do,

Lunch had been all the better because he had eaten in the company of the Dumble Dor. As soon as the fat beetle had plumped himself down at the table, the rest of the Council had made various hasty excuses, and promised to be back as soon as their very busy schedule would allow.

'It's the pong ,you know,' the Dumble Dor had explained cheerfully. 'It's no bed o' roses being a Dung beetle. They're such a fussy lot, most of them.'

Henry had decided he didn't mind the smell. It was no worse than his cousins' farm, and he had spent many happy, grubby hours there in the days before his parents had got interested in things.

'Well, I like the smell,' he had confided. The Dumble Dor had chuckled appreciatively.

'Well you're a boy after my own heart and no mistake,' he had said breathlessly. 'I just knew you and I would get on when I first set eyes on you. We'll show them a thing or two between us, I can tell you.'

Henry looked doubtful. 'To be perfectly honest, I didn't really follow what the Stag Beetle was saying most of the time,' he admitted.

There was a burst of loud chuckles from the Dumble Dor.

'Bless you lad - nobody ever does. He's a boring old beetle and no mistake. All his airs and graces and big words - I don't think he understands the half of it himself.'

'Do you think,' Henry asked timidly, 'you could fill in the gaps for me - just the bits I couldn't follow. After all, they do seem to be expecting so much from me, and if I haven't got a clue what it's about there's not much point in being the brave warrior, it seems to me.'

The Dumble Dor held up a hand. 'Food first,' he said firmly, and there followed half an hour of contented silence, broken only by the sounds of munching. Now while he waited for the Dumble Dor to recover from his after-lunch doze, Henry had the chance to examine at last, the sword which the Cardinal had presented him with such ceremony.

It was a beautiful weapon. The hilt and guard were crafted in gilded metal, and the lattice-work of the guard was encrusted with tiny jewels which stung the eyes as they sparkled in the bright sunshine. Carefully he drew it from its scabbard and felt the perfect balance of it in his hand - as though the sword smith had known the exact build and balance of its future owner.

Along the gleaming blade were those mysterious elfin letters which had puzzled him in his brief glance at them earlier. Henry stood up. A little under the shade, there was a tall plant with large, fleshy leaves. Henry sized up his target, then swung the sword in a whispering arc through the still air.

The plant was severed so effortlessly, that he almost fell under the force of the sweep. He took a hesitant step forward, aware of a faint musical ringing in his ears, long after the sweep of the flashing blade had come to rest.

'Careful my boy,' there was genuine alarm in the Dumble Dor's voice. 'That there's no toy. You listen to her song. It's the sword of a Prince, tempered by forgotten magicians of the sword smith's art. You draw it only when there' real work to be done.'

Sheepishly, Henry returned the sword to its studded scabbard. As he carefully pushed the bright blade home into the smooth sheath, he felt suddenly the silence that had fallen over the glade. The sword clicked home to the sound of birdsong and crickets again.

The Dumble Dor grinned at Henry's puzzlement. 'I think it's time you an' me took a little stroll,' he said. 'Easier to show you how things are than to waste time on long, boring stories from dusty books.'

'But what about the others?' Henry looked over his shoulder. Surely, he thought, they would be back any moment. The Stag Beetle had been most emphatic that the Council business was only just started. The Dumble Dor beckoned him over.

'Sit down my boy. Let me explain about that lot,' he said cheerfully, with a touch of scorn. Obediently, Henry sat at his side on the moss bank.

'The thing is,' said the Dumble Dor. 'They've probably forgotten all about you for the moment. Oh - they scuttle about in all the world of a hurry, and bossier than a busload of school teachers, but they can't keep anything in their heads for more than five minutes.'

'But they all seem so - important.'

'Not a bit of it. There's not an ounce of sense between them for all their airs and graces. See the butterflies,' he waved merrily to one which happened to be fluttering past. 'They're ripping them off left, right and centre. That ball last night - all the butterflies' idea - cost a gallon or two of nectar that did, I can tell you.'

'But what about the Watch Beetle?'

'Ah - he's a different kettle of fish altogether. Old Watch and me go back a long way - ever since we were grubs together. He's like me you see, slow but steady, and he's had to look after things all on his own all this time, while that lot's been running around having big ideas and then forgetting what they were five minutes later.'

'Matter of fact,' he continued, 'That's where I was going to take you now. I'm a simple sort, I am, and not very good at explaining. Old Watch will soon sort you out - mind you, he's going to be well put out when he finds out about last night's caper, I can tell you.'

All the time he had been talking, the Dumble Dor had been giving himself a thorough scratching, his voice muffled at times as he buried his head under his wing cases. Now he seemed satisfied, and he dusted himself down and lumbered off, with Henry at his side.

Henry stole a glance over his shoulder as they dived into the undergrowth.

The sunny glade was empty of life.

Had Henry been able to see the same spot a few minutes later, he would have witnessed a busy gathering of beetles, led by an anxious looking Cardinal. The Cardinal was waving all his arms about, obviously trying to make some point.

'But I tell you, I left him here, not much more than an hour ago.'

'In that case, where is he now?' The Stag Beetle was obviously not convinced.

'Well, if he wasn't here, why did we have all that dancing and stuff last night.... and I looked in the chest, and the sword's gone...... and anyway, I distinctly remember.....'

As the beetles argued long into the afternoon, the Dumble Dor and Henry arrived, in a remarkably short time, outside the towering walls of Barraclough House.

CHAPTER TEN

'I don't understand it,' Henry stared at the great wall in front of them. 'Yesterday, we walked for hours - and at such a pace too. Today, we're here in next to no time.'

The Dumble Dor snorted. 'Typical, typical. You see whet they're like - all of them the same. Probably going round in circles most of the time. Complete scatter brains.' He turned sharply to their left and began plodding along the base of the wall.

'Got to be a bit careful from now on,' he said loudly over his shoulder. 'We don't want to bump into one of their patrols. I'll take you in by one of the back ways.'

After a short walk, they arrived at an enormous grating, set in the massive red blocks of which the entire wall was composed. The grating was unfortunately a long distance above their heads, and the Dumble Dor stood for some moments in silence, thoughtfully scratching between its feelers. Then he turned to Henry, and eyed him up and down doubtfully.

'Fact is,' he confided. 'I usually take a bit of a run-up from over there, and fly this bit,' an idea struck him.

'I don't suppose,' he said hopefully, 'that you could *fall* up there?'

Henry explained with regret that falling was really only a downward thing. The Dumble Dor was clearly not impressed.

'Seems a bit limited to me,' he said doubtfully. 'I mean, how do you get back up again when you've finished?'

'I think I might be able to climb up there,' said Henry. 'There are plenty of handholds and footholds. You could go on and wait for me at the top.'

The Dumble Dor took him at his word, and Henry stood in the shadow of the wall while the fat beetle carefully paced out his run-up, to a considerable distance out towards the shrubbery. Then began the process of flying, which, if it had seemed laboured in the Watch Beetle, became a positive pantomime in the hands of the Dumble Dor.

It started with a variety of limbering up exercises, and the elaborate unfurling of a set of surprising gossamer wings, which he tucked outwards from under his wing cases like someone assembling a large kite.

'I'm not too keen on this flying thing,' called the beetle, by way of explanation. 'Matter of fact, I tend to close my eyes a bit.' he confided.

As Henry watched, the flimsy wings began vibrating ever faster and faster, setting up a loud droning noise. Soon the beetle was hopping up and down, each hop carrying him a little higher than the last, as though on an invisible trampoline. Finally with a loud grunt, he left the ground completely, and began buzzing through the air in a shallow arc in the general direction of the grating. There was a loud clunk, as he hit the wall squarely, about a foot to the right of the opening.

Henry held his breath as the Dumble Dor spiralled earthwards, but at the last moment, within inches of the ground, he suddenly gathered himself again, and soared upwards once more. This time he succeeded in hitting the target, and fell dustily through one of the gaps in the grating. He sat on the edge of the opening, puffing and wheezing, and began furling the kite of gossamer to tuck it back under the wing cases.

'Flying's for younger chaps than me, I reckon,' He called down to Henry, as his breath returned. 'Still, I can have a rest while you follow me up. Up you come, while I have a bit of a lie down up here.' Henry faced the wall and began to climb, flattening himself against the uneven surface. The climb was much longer than it had looked from ground level, and he made slow and nervous progress, feeling for handholds above him and then dragging himself painfully upwards. He had completed half the climb when the Dumble Dor suddenly hissed down at him.

'Stop there a moment my boy - just don't move!' there was no mistaking the urgency of the command. Henry pulled himself even more tightly against the wall, wishing that he had been able to secure a tighter hold on the crack above his head.

'What's the matter', he whispered back, not daring to look up or down.

'Patrol coming. Don't move until they've gone past, and they won't notice you. They never look up.'

Henry heard the sound of approaching footsteps, stepping out in the military rhythm of a march. There were other sounds too, a sort of mixture of clanking and squeaking sounds which seemed to keep to the same rhythm. Henry felt an overwhelming curiosity to see what the cause of the sounds was.

Cautiously, he craned his neck round, trying to get a view of the ground beneath, but it was impossible without leaning dangerously out from the wall.

The sounds approached closer still, and now he could hear a harsh, tinny voice snapping out commands.

"Eft, right, - 'eft, right, 'eft....'

Henry's fingers were now beginning to ache and tremble as he hooked them desperately over the ledge above him. He had been on the point of bringing his foot up to the next foothold, so that his position now on the face of the wall, was with arms and legs at full stretch, and he was tiring rapidly.

'Hang on lad - won't be long now,' the Dumble Dor hissed from above him. Henry hung on.

The marchers passed directly below him as his arms now began to tremble under the strain. Henry closed his eyes tightly and clenched his teeth tightly, trying to fight against the ache, but it was no good. Slowly, but surely, his fingers were beginning to slip form the precarious hold on the ledge.

'Halt!'

To Henry's horror, the sounds of marching ceased abruptly. They had stopped almost directly below him. Henry imagined their eyes boring into his back, and was struck with panic. Whoever they were, they must now, he thought be staring directly up at him, spread-eagled above them on the wall.

His head was swimming now - the pain in his fingers unbearable. He tried to look up to where the Dumble Dor must be waiting anxiously, but he was unable to move his head for fear of dislodging himself. What terrible weapons, he wondered must be even now trained on his unprotected back?

There was a clank from below, followed by a shouted command which he couldn't make out. Henry braced himself. Then, to his relief, the sounds of marching began again.

Henry let out a long sigh, and for the second time in two days - he fell.

CHAPTER ELEVEN

Henry landed with a bump which, for a moment, shook all the breath out of his body.

The first thing he noticed, as he recovered his breath, was that he seemed miraculously unhurt. Something soft had broken his fall.

The second thing he realised was that, equally miraculously, his fall had gone un-noticed by the patrol. Henry sat up cautiously and looked in the direction of their retreating backs.

They were a strange sight.

What he saw was a column of figures, marching like mechanical toys, two abreast away from him along the foot of the wall. They were dressed in shining black armour from head to toe, and this seemed to be the source of the clanking and squeaking. Each head was encased in a round helmet, above which there protruded a pair of slender feelers which swayed in rhythm to their march. The upper part of the armour bulged dramatically, only to dwindle to almost nothing at the waist. The lower part also curved sharply outwards, then faded to a sharp pointed tail, which wagged jerkily behind them. Each of them was walking on two pairs of spindly legs, the left, then the right moving together in an exaggerated march step.

The sight was so comical, that Henry found it difficult not to burst out laughing as the little group gradually disappeared into the distance. As they reached the far corner of the building, he faintly heard the tinny command ringing back to him.

"Igt wheeeeel!' and at last they were gone, and he felt safe to stand up and take stock of his surroundings.

'You all right my boy?' the Dumble Dor called anxiously from his perch in the grating.

'I think so - I landed on something soft,' as he said it, Henry realised that the 'something soft' was actually a coil of rope, tucked in near the shrubbery which stood close to the wall. Henry picked up the heavy rope and examined it excitedly. It was a sort of orange twine, like the kind used to tie bales, but like everything else which belonged to that other world beyond Henry's strange and tiny self, it was enormously bulky, so that it was only with difficulty that he was able to heft it over his shoulder and carry it to the base of the wall.

'I've found a rope,' he called up to the waiting beetle. 'I'm going to throw it up, so you can tie it to the grating.'

It was a difficult task, throwing up the rope. The first time it fell pitifully short of the target, and on the second occasion, the Dumble Dor was too slow to catch the coil as it bumped into the grating at his side. Finally, however, the rope was firmly secured, and in no time at all, Henry had shinned up to join his friend on the ledge outside the grating. He sat there for a moment getting his breath back.

'I still can't believe that they didn't hear me fall,' he said to the beetle, who was fumbling with the knot of the rope. 'I thought I was going to land on top of them.'

'You'd have had to land on top of them before they noticed you,' the beetle replied with cheerful contempt. 'I told you they never looked up - they never look anywhere at all, as a matter of fact, except straight ahead when they're marching. Frightening enough, I dare say, if they was coming straight at you, but old Watch and myself have followed them for miles before now, and they haven't had the slightest idea we were there.'

'So are all the ants like that?'

'That lot's just the soldiers. Not very bright any of them, but they work together - it's all training with them. There's others you might need to be more worried about, but Watch can explain better than me.' and the Dumble Dor heaved on the last remnant of the rope, which now lay neatly coiled behind the grating. Then he set off down yet another ragged passage which led away from the grating into the house.

Following him, Henry found himself once again inside the skeleton of Barraclough House. At the time when the house had been built, after the bricklayers, the plasterers, the carpenters had finished their work, they had left behind them a honeycomb of tunnels and passages to be colonised by hordes of unofficial tenants from the surrounding countryside.

Since that time, there had been occasional intrusions into that secret world, as electricians had come to leave their long, sagging loops of heavy cable, plumbers had cluttered the passageways with massive, resonating pipes, but for the most part, it had remained a world beyond the reach of human exploration, safe in the hands of its tiny lodgers.

Henry would never have suspected that, beyond the heavily varnished skirting boards and faded, flaking plaster of Barraclough House, this different and exciting world could have existed.

It was clear to him now, as he followed the Dumble Dor's wide, lumbering back, that these passages had been well-used over the years. The roadways had long ago been cleared of the debris with which the workmen had felt no need to concern themselves, hidden as it was forever from the human gaze. Even, at crossings of the ways, there were signposts, written in the strange, angular lettering which he had failed to read on the blade of his sword.

It was equally clear to him that this was a world which had now been abandoned. Nothing else moved in the passage ways, and there was a hollow, echoing emptiness about the place of the kind which falls on all buildings which have been abandoned by their inhabitants.

Only once on their long journey did they see signs of life. Henry heard ahead of them, the now familiar sound of an approaching patrol. They ducked into a side turning and watched them pass, each jerky, mechanical movement exactly in step, and the eyes fixed firmly and unswervingly, directly ahead. So confident was the Dumble Dor, that as the last shining figure clanked and squeaked past the opening of the side passage, he simply stepped out again to continue his leisurely shambling pace in their wake.

'Soon be there now, lad.' he said conversationally over his shoulder, not even bothering to lower his voice as it echoed down the corridor.

'Aren't you afraid they'll hear us?' asked Henry nervously, watching the retreating patrol dwindle ahead of them.

'Clank, clank, squeak, squeak,' said the beetle. 'If you jumped out and shouted 'boo!' I don't think they'd spot you - not unless they bumped into you, that is.'

Finally they came to a halt. Henry saw that a set of shallow steps had been cut into the wall of the passageway, leading upwards. The Dumble Dor clambered up, and Henry followed to find himself moments later in a spacious room which led off the tunnel through a low doorway.

The room was filled with light and warmth, both provided by a fire which was burning brightly at the far end of the room. Next to the fire, in a comfortable easy chair, sat the Watch Beetle, reading a heavy book by the light of the blaze. Henry turned to his guide.

'Where are we?' he whispered, at a loss to understand the fire.

'Back of the kitchen stove,' was the reply. 'Watch has lived here for years- ants or no ants.' and without ceremony, he waddled across the room and plumped himself down in a second easy chair opposite the Watch Beetle.

'The Watch Beetle sniffed. 'Hallo Dumble,' he said without looking up from his book. 'So you brought the boy back then? You took your time.'

'Well, I thought that lot out there would only turn his head with all their nonsense - and he's got work to do, hasn't he?'

'Yes indeed,' the Watch Beetle turned to look critically at Henry, who began to feel rather nervous under his gaze. 'Does he understand?' he asked cryptically.

'Some of it, I think. But you can explain better than I can.'

The Watch Beetle motioned Henry to a third chair, next to his own and slowly set aside his book.

'Well Henry,' Henry started to hear hid name used for the first time. 'Let me tell you how things are.'

CHAPTER TWELVE

'Well, young man, I expect you feel we've got a pretty easy life from what you've seen so far?'

Henry admitted that he could see little cause for any of the beetles he had met to plead hardship.

'I thought as much. They've really laid thing on for you , I expect - given you the long-lost Prince routine; but of course, they've got it all wrong as usual. Now what happened yesterday after I left.

Henry explained about the ball and the costume and the food, his face aglow at the memory of it. The Watch Beetle snorted.

'Garden gnomes - typical! I wonder where they got those from. You see, just when you want them to be sensible and get on with things, they go and throw a party. Now what about the Council meeting - I asked them to hold a Council meeting. Though that at least might wake them up a bit.'

Once again Henry related the events of that morning. 'It all seemed very important,' he finished rather lamely.

'Oh yes, I'm sure they made it *seem* important - and now they've gone off and forgotten all about you. If it wasn't for old Dumble here....' the Watch Beetle broke off, shaking his head. 'Oh well, it can't be helped,' he continued eventually. 'and I don't suppose we'll ever change them...' again he lapsed into silence. He was looking at Henry closely, taking in the now rather crumpled battledress.

'I see they've given you the sword of the Scarab too - all very impressive, but it's not the answer, you know.'

'The answer to what?' asked Henry. It was all very well, he thought, for the Watch Beetle to complain at him, but really it was all nothing to do with him. He was beginning to feel once again, rather cross.

'Quite right - you want me to get on with it,' smiled the Watch Beetle '- been messed about enough, I dare say. Well then - this is what its about.' and he settled back in his chair and began to tell Henry the history of the Beetles of Barraclough House.

'Many year ago,' the beetle began. 'when this house was young, it was home to all of us. Oh, we had the woodlands around, and in Summer, it was fine to be out under the stars; but when the snows are on the ground, and its blowing a gale, it's a different story, and we were all glad of this place where we could find warmth and comfort, and a bite to eat.'

'At the start, we all lived quite happily - after all, there's plenty of room for everyone. It was an easy arrangement. You found your bit of space, and that's where you lived, and if your friends wanted to live there too, they moved in, and there was always plenty of room for the others. We shared what we found, and there was generally a good living to be had, in the kitchens and such.'

'Pretty soon though, they started their airs and graces, and trying to say that some of them deserved better places than others. We'd always been able to gather things from out there - quietly at night. We would look for things which would be useful to us - turn them into improvements like this,' he patted the chair, then with a sweeping gesture, indicated the other furnishings of his comfortable room.

'Then some of them took to collecting trinkets - coins, jewellery - anything which shone. It was useless stuff, all of it, and a heavy labour to collect, but it made them feel important, I suppose.'

'At last, they'd got so wrapped up in their nonsense about who was the most important, that they lost sight of the real threat to their whole silly existence. That's why all these corridors are empty now - that's why they've had to move their silly games out into the wide open woods again. They're all out there, just playing along and waiting for the winter to end it all.'

At this point, the Dumble Dor, who had seemed to doze through the Watch Beetle's story came abruptly to life.

'You see, my boy,' he said excitedly. 'It's like I told you. The ants - they just kicked us all out!'

The Watch Beetle frowned him into silence.

'They're not like us, the ants,' he continued. 'They've always been organised. A funny set-up, it seemed to us. They had their leaders and they had their groups of soldiers and workers and so on. We were content to ignore them, and they kept to their own part of the house, so that our paths never really crossed. But all the time we were playing our games, they were getting more and more organised, until one day they sent a messenger...'

'messenger!' the Dumble Dor exploded. 'Jumped up little pip-squeak> I should have bitten his head off there and then.'

'They gave us until the following day to move out. There was no longer enough room for us and them, they said, their numbers had increased so much. If we didn't go, it would be war, and they would over-run us all.'

'So what happened?' Henry was enthralled. This was something like an adventure.

'Well, needless to say, the Council had to hold a meeting to decide what to do, and they argued long into the night. By the time they'd decided that they didn't know what to do, most of the other beetles had already packed their bags and gone. When the ants sent a patrol round the house the next day, the Council just scuttled off after the rest of them into the woods - and there they've stayed, waiting for someone else to sort it all out.'

'But you're still here.' said Henry.

'Yes, well old Dumble and I, we decided to stay. Somebody had to keep an eye on the place after all.'

'But the ants - why haven't they attacked you - driven you out?'

'Oh they know I'm here right enough; but I don't think they ever intended things to come to a fight. They're not bad fellows one to one - not much in their heads, and absolutely no sense of humour - it's just when they get together like that you see.'

'But where do I fit in to all this?' Henry asked. The Beetle hesitated.

'Well,' he said finally. 'I want you to go and talk to them. None of this 'leading your people into battle against a common foe' stuff. I want you to talk to them. You're neither one of our kind nor one of theirs, so it might work.'

'But what if it doesn't?' Henry was beginning to feel distinctly nervous at the prospect of going alone down those echoing corridors to talk to an unknown enemy.

'That's an eventuality we'll have to plan for in advance,' said the Watch Beetle. 'Now I suggest we eat-' the Duimble Dor brightened noticeably at the prospect. 'Then we can get down to some serious work.'

He heaved himself out of the armchair and led the way to the table.

CHAPTER THIRTEEN

Henry was frightened. No two ways about it.

As he walked slowly down the dusty, sloping tunnel, deeper below Barraclough House, his heart was pounding uncomfortably, and he could feel sweat breaking out on his forehead in spite of the chill which hung in the air here below the foundations of the house.

The last time he'd felt like this in fect, was when he had been stood outside Mr. Waters, the Head's study on that occasion when he had been persuaded, against his better judgement to set off a fire extinguisher.

He felt his sword bumping at his side with each step, but he could take no comfort from it. He had never wielded a real sword, and the games which he had played with the long, straight twigs pruned from the apple trees in late Autumn, seemed to hold no promise that he could handle the blade in a real battle.

The Watch Beetle had, form the star, tried to discourage him from bringing the sword.

'You're supposed to be going to talk to them. A sword will only make them suspicious,' he had said; but eventually he had given in to Henry, who had felt at the Time that the sword would lend him some authority with this army. Only now his impulse seemed ridiculous. After all, he was far more likely to fall over the sword than anything else if it came to a real fight.

The tunnel which he was following was narrower than those higher up in the carcass of Barraclough House. He had spent some time with the Watch Beetle and the Dumble Dor, working his way around the upper levels, to get a clearer idea of the layout.

'There's a pattern, you see,' the Watch Beetle had explained. 'It repeats itself on each level of the house. Only it gets narrower as you go deeper.'

Henry had asked him why the ants had stayed in the lower levels. Why hadn't they simply taken over the whole place in the absence of the beetles?

'That's exactly it,' had been the terse reply. 'They don't need these levels, you see, nor do they particularly want them. That's why I think you could talk them out of this nonsense, if you could get to someone sensible down there.'

It had all sounded so straightforward when the Watch Beetle had said it, up there in the warmth and comfort of his room behind the kitchen stove. Down here it was different, and Henry waited at any moment for hordes of armed soldier ants to leap out on him with drawn swords.

There was much more activity down here than on the upper levels. There, it had been all dust and silence, and the solitary echo of their footsteps. Down here he found himself frequently having to duck aside into one of the many Side e tunnels, to avoid a clanking, squeaking patrol. In the light of day, outside the walls, their mechanical progress had seemed comical. Down here in the shadows, it was a sinister and frightening procession, and he was amazed that they didn't hear his pounding heart even above the clanking of their armour.

Carefully following the Watch Beetle's directions, Henry went on down towards the cellars of Barraclough House. He had to count his way past the various side openings, all the time afraid that he would make a mistake, and be lost forever in this underground maze.

'Don't worry.' the Watch Beetle had said brightly. 'Old Dumble and I know every inch of this place. If you do get lost, you've just got to sit tight till we find you. We won't be far behind, remember.'

Henry tried d to find some comfort in the Watch Beetle's words, but it somehow didn't stop him feeling terribly alone at the moment. In an effort to shake off his fear, he cast his mind back to the exploration of the upper levels of the house which they had made before his departure.

It had been a voyage of discovery for Henry. In room after room, he saw common little household objects put to quite different uses in this miniature world. In one, there was a magnificent banqueting table, which had once seen service as a wooden kitchen tray. The set of silver serving dished, he instantly recognised as upturned thimbles, but he was at first at a loss to identify the tableware, until he realised that the side plates were made from drawing-pins without their points, and the main dishes, carefully polished milk bottle tops. The Watch Beetle dismissed it all with a comptemptful gesture.

'See what I mean?' he had said. 'Nonsense, all of it. No wonder they got kicked out -Banqueting Hall, I ask you!'

The biggest surprise had been the Council Chamber itself, all pomp and wood panelling, with a heavy chair set on a raised platform at the front. It was the wall behind the chair however, that held Henry spellbound.

'That's one of my old paintings,' he said in amazement.

Sure enough, in a heavy, patterned frame, there hung above the chair, a picture of what was supposed to be a person. It was a child's drawing, the body a long, oval blob, and the arms and legs added on afterwards like cocktail sticks in a potato. Even for the five year old he must have been when the painting was made, it was not, Henry decided, one of his better efforts.

'What's it doing here?' he asked, bewildered.

'There you are you see,' the Watch Beetle pointed to the neat, angular print under the picture. 'Portrait of the Prince, it says.'

Henry felt rather flattered to have his picture hung in what was so obviously an important place, but he thought better of saying anything to his companions, who were evidently quite disgusted with all these ceremonial trappings.

Eventually they had returned to the Watch Beetle's comfortable quarters, and had spent what turned out to be a most agreeable evening, working out a plan of campaign. It had all seemed so easy then - the threat somehow so distant and minor. Henry had good cause to remember his courageous talk of the night before, as he stood quaking in the chill corridor, trying to summon up the strength to carry on.

The Watch beetle and the Dumble Dor had obviously waited a long time for his arrival. They were full of plans and counter-plans, which should take care of every contingency. It was late in the night before they had suggested a bite of supper, and Henry's head was, by then, ringing with all the instructions.

Supper had been eaten in those comfortable armchairs by the cheerful fire, and had been followed by a small crystal glass full of the delightful nectar which Henry had sampled on the day of the ball.

'The butterflies,' The Watch Beetle had explained.' It's about the only good thing they produce. The bees aren't a patch on them.'

Finishing his glass, Henry was instantly drowsy, and when the other two showed him to the bed which had been made up in a corner of the room, he fell into instant, dreamless sleep, secure in the company of his new friends, who dozed contentedly in their armchairs by the glowing embers of the fire.

He had been woken early by the Dumbvle Dor, who had brought

him a small bowl of the same liquid which had refreshed and enlivened him before the meeting of the Council.

There had followed a further session of training in the upper levels of the house, before they had wished him luck, and his real mission had begun.

Now he was struggling to remember the exact instructions.

He had reached a point in the tunnel where there was a sharp fork, one passage leading on downwards, the other sloping steeply up again. Henry took the upward path and was soon puffing and panting with the effort of the climb.

Finally, the tunnel halted abruptly. He was in almost total darkness here, and he had to feel around ahead for the rough door which he knew he should expect to find in the wall.

Fumbling for the latch, he cautiously swung the door inwards towards him, wary of any creaking of hinges.

He stepped through, pulling it gently shut behind him, and his courage almost failed him completely at the sight which met him there.

He was finally in the kingdom of the ants.

CHAPTER FOURTEEN

Henry flattened himself against the rough wall of the passage, feeling suddenly dizzy and faint.

He was high up on a narrow ledge, above a vast, square cavern. What part of the structure of Barraclough House it might have formed, he could not imagine, but it was evidently the headquarters of the ant population.

The floor of the cavern was lit with a series of smoky fires, which gave the whole thing a strange, eerie red glow. In the light of the fires, under the drifting, oily smoke, he could see that the cavern floor was laid out in symmetrical rows with some sort of huts or tents. At their centre was what was obviously a parade ground, and as he watched, a whole battalion of ants was marching endlessly up and down with absolute precision.

Faintly, he could hear the tinny bark of commands as, reaching the further limit of the parade ground, the serried ranks wheeled smartly in unison, to begin the steady march back again.

Henry had never had a head for heights. Once, his father had taken him up to the top of the lighthouse on a visit to Plymouth Hoe. Henry had struggled manfully up the steps, but once outside on the platform around the lamp-housing, he had stayed pinned against the wall, tight-lipped with terror. His father had never been one to accept signs of weakness. He had coaxed him to the edge, to wave to his mother, and Henry had stood, staring glassily at the minute figures far below.

Now, as then, he was gripped with the same p[panic - that feeling that, in spite of all his mental efforts, the irresistible urge to jump would catch hold of him, and he would be hurled into nothingness. Looking down, he felt himself drawn towards the drop as though by an invisible hand, and he shrank back further against the wall.

One of the fires which lit the underground world was directly below Henry's perch. The smoke drifter upwards, stinging his eyes. It had a strange smell to it, but it was a smell which was also oddly familiar. Henry recognised it suddenly as the stench which Uncle Jimmy always dismissed with the word 'drains'.

If nothing else, the discomfort of the smoke helped to overcome his fear of the drop, and he was soon scuttling, crab-like along the narrow ledge, alert to any sign from below that he had been spotted. He tried to find comfort in the Dumble Dor's words.

'They never look up.'

The beetle was evidently quite right about the ants. The machine-like precision of the drill continued unaltered, as he made his way along the ledge to the point where the tunnel resumed on the other side.

This tunnel, so the Watch Beetle had told him, was an old passageway down to the quarters where the Queen of the ants held court.

'It's no good trying to talk to the others,' the beetle had said. 'They all follow orders. They probably won't understand what you're talking about. No - you've got to go straight to the top, It's the Queen you've got to find.'

So Henry with great caution and a rapidly beating heart, entered the tunnel on the other side of the cavern, and quietly tip-toed down to the entrance door at the far end which would lead him to the ante-room of the Queen's chamber. He knew just where the door would be, around a slight bend in the tunnel. The Watch Beetle had told him. Henry hurried around the corner, anxious to get on with his mission while his courage held. He stopped in his tracks.

One thing, he realised, the Watch Beetle had not known.

The doorway was guarded.

Two tall, frightening figures in shining black armour stood, one on either side of the door. Before he could turn and run, one of them had spotted him.

"Alt!' snapped the guard. 'OOgoes there!' It stopped for a moment and, fumbling amongst the chain mail on its bulging chest, it brought out a much-thumbed pocket book which it consulted closely, squinting in the dim light.

'Friend or foe!' it recited eventually. The other guard watched approvingly without moving from its post next to the door.

'Friend, of course,' said Henry tremulously, trying to sound confident.

The ant looked at him for a moment, then began flicking through the pages of the book again. Finally it said:

'Pass, friend,' and stood smartly to one side, its spear at the slope. Henry stepped forward, repressing a strong impulse to turn and run. Suddenly the other guard came to life, barring his way.

"Ang on a minute, Bert,' it said reproachfully. 'You don't know if its tellin' the truth.' Bert frowned, trying to grasp this difficult idea.

'But 'e *said* friend,' he said eventually. The second guard took a step towards the terrified boy and spoke confidentially behind the back of a metal-gloved hand.

'You'll 'ave to fergive Bert, mate - only we've never 'ad nobody come 'ere before. Been standing 'ere for weeks and weeks too,' he added glumly. Then an idea struck him.

'Tell you what,' he said. 'You juss wait 'ere a minute an' I'll 'ave a conflab wiv me colleague 'ere'.

He left Henry standing rooted in puzzlement as much as fear, while he stepped back for an earnest, muttered consultation with the other ant guard. Henry heard the word 'password' mentioned several times in a hoarse whisper. Then the second ant stepped back to him.

'give the day's password.' he said importantly.

'I need to see the Queen,' Henry pleaded. The ant looked at him doubtfully.

'I don't think that's it,' he said looking over his shoulder. 'Is that it, Bert?'

'Nah,' Bert's voice was triumphant. 'Nothing like it. It says 'ere today's password is Batter Pudding.'

'Bert!'

To Henry's amazement, the second ant stepped smartly back to the first and began slapping him across the head with the back of his glove. A series of loud clangs echoed down the corridor. Eventually he stopped, exhausted. The first ant stuck its fingers in its ears and shook its head vigorously.

'Whassamarrer?' it asked eventually in a dazed voice> The second ant was full of scorn.

'Matter? I'll tell you what the matter is. You've only gorn an' given away today's password. Don' you realise what that means?'

The first ant evidently didn't' It was too busy trying to stem the ringing in its ears.

'It means,' continued the second ant, with solemn emphasis,' That this creature 'ere can walk up to us any time for the rest of today - can juss walk up to us an' give us the password, an' we'll let 'im through - that's what it means, that's what you've gorn an' done.' and the first ant's helmet clanged again under the blows of the glove.

Henry saw his chance. Quickly, he ducked back again around the corner and waited.

'Where'd 'e go?' he heard the first ant ask.

''E done a runner,' answered the second, a note of relief in its voice.

''Adn't we better go after 'im?' the first ant sounded doubtful.

'Nah,' the answer was emphatic. 'It says in the daily orders that we gotta guard this door, and that's what we'll do.'

Henry waited a moment, then stepped smartly back round the corner to confront the guards, who sprang to attention once again.

''OO goes there - friend or foe?' the first ant was getting the hang of things now.

'Friend.' said Henry simply.

'Password for the day,' demanded the first ant threateningly.

'Batter Pudding,' said Henry.

'Pass, friend,' said the first ant smartly. Heels clicking, they stood stiffly aside, and Henry passed through the imposing door into the palace of the queen.

CHAPTER FIFTEEN

Once beyond the heavy, studded door, Henry found himself suddenly at a loss. I mean, after all - you couldn't just walk up to a Queen and start talking to her just like anyone else. In any case, to tell the truth, he really still hadn't any idea how he would find her. The Watch Beetle and the Dumble Dor had known exactly how to find the way as far as the back entrance to the palace, but they had never themselves set foot beyond that door. He was entirely on his own from now on, and the thought left him cold with anxiety.

'Calm down,' he said to himself aloud. 'Get the lie of the land first. There's plenty of time.'

He began looking around the large and mercifully empty room into which the two guards had so readily admitted him.

This was evidently the guardroom of the palace. It was lit by a series of strangely-shaped lamps, hung from massive brackets around the walls, and giving off the same dense, oily smoke that had caused his eyes to water out on the ledge, so that the vast room was full of eerie flickering shadows, out of which there loomed shining suits of jet-black armour, to make him start in alarm.

All along the walls were ranged racks of weapons - ugly, curved swords, long, slender pikes and double-headed battle axes. No wonder, thought Henry, that the muddle-headed beetles had fled before the threat of this formidable enemy.

Henry drew one of the swords from its place in the rack and tried its balance. It was a heavy, clumsy thing, quite unlike the bright, bejewelled weapon which hung at his side, but he imagined several thousand of these blades in the well-trained hands of the ant army, and could not repress a shudder at the picture it conjured up of a terrible destruction wrought on the helpless beetles.

He was carefully returning the sword to its place among the ranks, when he suddenly froze in horror. There was a loud rattle at the massive door to the guard room.

Someone was coming.

Henry had no time to think. He ran the length of the room and threw open a smaller, less imposing door which he had noticed in the shadows at the far end. Whatever was beyond it, it was better than waiting here for certain capture.

Beyond the door, he found himself in another maze of tunnels, and in panic, he chose one at random and hurried down it. At each branch, he tried to keep in his head a mental record of the turnings which he had taken, but at the end of some five minutes, he had to admit to himself that he was thoroughly and hopelessly lost. There was no hope of the beetles finding him here. Nothing for it then, but to press on and hope that eventually, he would find his way by accident out of the maze.

There was a further problem too. The longer he walked, the darker the tunnels became. Soon Henry was feeling his way along the walls, wary of what lay ahead in the darkness, and once again fighting back the impulse to panic., He was near tears now - nothing like the brave warrior who had set out on this adventure a few hours earlier. Henry had become a lost and very small boy in the threatening darkness, and he would have welcomed even capture by the ants, if only it would mean rescue from this nightmare.

He had drawn his sword, and was waving it in front of him, as a blind man waves his stick, feeling for the sides of the tunnel ahead, searching for any unevenness in the floor. Finally, the sword tip encountered empty space to his left. There was another tunnel branching off from the one in which he felt imprisoned. Crouching down, he felt the edges of the opening. They were smooth and rounded, like a large pipe. As he squatted there, Henry was suddenly sure that he could hear faint sounds, coming from somewhere far off. It was a very faint, but distinct snoring sound, echoing up through the pipe.

After the black emptiness of the tunnel, any sign of life seemed to Henry like salvation. He sheathed his sword and stepped into the pipe.

And slipped.

Like a crazy helter-skelter, the pie whisked Henry downwards, the wind rushing through his hair. Henry closed his eye tight and let out a long wail of terror. Then, as suddenly as it had begun, his ride ended.

'Oooooooooff!'

He had landed on something soft and yielding, and from there he bounced into an untidy heap on the floor, which seemed to be covered with some silken material. As he struggled to his feet, Henry realised with a shock that he was not alone.

'Well **REALLY!**' The voice was full of outrage. It held exactly the same tone that his Great Aunt Emily had used on the occasion when she had discovered him sheepishly climbing out of her ornamental pond.

'How **DARE** you!' said the voice, as Henry got tangled with his sword and landed once again in a heap on the silken floor.

'What on earth are you?' the voice asked. Henry finally found his feet, and stood staring at the apparition before him.

There could be no doubt about it - he was finally in the presence of the Queen.

Henry burst into tears........

'There, there now, ducky - don't take on so,' Henry found himself suddenly gripped in a vast motherly embrace, his head patted in sympathy.

'There's no real harm done. I expect you were just playing,' the voice continued soothingly. 'Boys will be boys - I should know, I've got eighteen thousand nine hundred and forty-three of them.' Henry stopped crying in astonishment. Surely his ears must be playing tricks with him.

'Did you say eighteen thousand nine hundred and forty-three?' he gasped.

'That's right dearie - boys that is. Not so many girls I'm afraid. they're ever so much easier on the whole girls are,' she confided 'No offence mind....'

As she rambled on, Henry was able fully to appreciate the strange figure before him. The Queen was a monstrous figure, twenty times the size of the biggest of the soldier ants. Her huge abdomen was swathed in a pink flannel night-dress, and she was reclining on a bed covered in equally pink silken draperies. As she spoke she rubbed absently with one of her arms at the spot which had broken Henry's fall. Henry, his tears now completely forgotten, was trying to remember that it was rude to stare.

'Tell you what,' The Queen continued. 'We could visit some of the girls if you like. I hardly ever get out much nowadays. It'd do me good to shoe you round the nursery.'

'That is indeed gracious of you, your majesty,' said Henry, bowing and hoping to set the right tone. He had never spoken to Royalty before. He was answered by a bellow of laughter which shook the silken draperies of the monstrous bed.

'Your majesty -your majesty. OOh that's rich. Careful or I'll split my sides.' The Queen actually rolled about in her mirth. Henry blushed.

The Queen noticed his embarrassment, and the heaving subsided.

'I'm sorry, dearie, but it's just what you said. Struck me as funny. You are a scream, really you are.'

'But what *do* I call you then,' asked a puzzled Henry.

'Call me Queenie of course - same as everybody else. They all call me Queenie.'

'In that case - ' Henry gulped. '_Queenie,' he continued bravely, 'I'd love to look around the nursery with you.'

'Right you are then,' said the Queen, and she turned to the door.

'Declan, Damien!' she shouted.

The door swung open and two tall guards in full, shining armour appeared. They stood staring menacingly at Henry, their long, vicious lances gleaming in the lamplight.

CHAPTER SIXTEEN

The Queen leaned her massive bulk over towards the frightened boy.

'I'm afraid I didn't catch your name,' she said in a polite whisper.

'Henry,' stammered Henry, trying not to squeak. The Queen turned to the guards.

'Declan - Damien, this is Henry. He's a friend of mine. Henry, this is Declan 253 and Damien 76' once again, her bulk leaned confidingly towards him.

'Have to give them numbers,' she whispered. 'Ran out of names long ago. Ever so hard to remember sometimes.' Henry was too busy watching Declan and Damien's lances to take it all in. The Queen turned back to the guards.

'Now put those things away,' she said briskly, flapping an arm in the direction of the weapons. 'and go and fetch my carriage. I'm taking Henry on a tour of the nursery.'

Declan shuffled uncomfortably. 'But Mum,' he hesitated. 'Do you really think you should?'

Damien looked sulky.

'We was given orders to guard you,' he faltered. The Queen's expression became suddenly severe.

'And I'm giving you orders to fetch my carriage,' she said firmly. 'I've told you before about this soldiers business. Just remember who you are talking to young man.'

The two guards shamefacedly dropped their weapons and left

hastily on their errand.

'Soldiers, soldiers all the time with some of them,' the Queen said cheerfully. ' I think the Damiens and the Declans are the worst - mind you, come to think of it the Adrians and Andrews are just as bad really. Now just you help me up, dearie, and we'll go and have a look around - I'm looking forward to this. You've put new life into me, I can tell you.'

With some difficulty, Henry helped the Queen to her feet, and she waddles with much puffing and panting to the door. Outside stood an open carriage, drawn by a squad of six ants in livery. The Queen hauled herself aboard, and patted the few remaining centimetres of seat at her side.

'Climb up, Henry - we'll start with a tour of the Dairy,' she called cheerfully. The ants took the strain as Henry clambered aboard, and with much grunting and groaning on their part, they were off.

The first port of call as promised, was the Dairy. The carriage drove slowly and sedately down the central aisle, while the Queen pointed out the two regular rows of green aphids, which stood contentedly munching their leaves, each in an individual stall, just like the cows at Henry's cousin's farm. At each aphid there was an ant, busily milking, and a further squad of ants moved along the rows, collecting the full containers of aphids' milk and carrying them off out of the dairy on wooden yokes.

These ants, Henry noticed, were dressed quite differently from the dreaded guards. Their skins had less lustre, and they seemed smaller somehow, without the menace of the shining armour. Every now and then, the Queen would halt the carriage, with an imperious tap of the long, thin cane which she carried, and would lean out to address the workers, the carriage sagging dangerously as she did so.

'Hello Norman, Albert - this is Henry,' and the ants would stop their busy activity for a moment to give a cheerful wave.

'What friendly people,' thought Henry, and was a little ashamed to feel surprised at the thought.

Finally the Dairy tour was over, and the Queen turned to him, smiling.

'Now you must meet the grubs,' she said. 'You'll have to keep quiet so as not to wake them though.'

Henry nodded agreement, and the carriage lumbered laboriously on until they found themselves in a strange gallery, the walls of which were lined with pigeon-holes. As they moved slowly down the gallery, Henry realised that each pigeon-hole was occupied by a large wriggling white grub. the worker ants were busy here, ladling the products of the milkers into the wide open mouths of the squirming, glutinous infants.

The Queen halted the carriage once more and gazed lovingly at the wriggling masses before her.

'Aren't they just *gorgeous*?' she asked expansively.

Henry just managed to nod.

'That's Penelope up there,' continued the Queen, indicating a particularly large specimen with a mouth like a vacuum cleaner. 'I have great hopes for Penelope. And that one there is Sadie 57, and that's Julie 33 and Samantha 28 - such nice grubs.' she concluded.

Henry was speechless. How could she tell them apart, he wondered.

'But I see you're tired,' continued the Queen, noticing Henry's gaping mouth. 'To tell the truth, I'm a little weary myself with all this excitement. Let's go and have a bite to eat, and then perhaps you can tell me a bit about yourself<' and she gave him a dig in the ribs which threatened to expel him from the carriage. 'After all - you were a bit of a surprise, weren't you?'

'Yes -I 'd rather drop in on you,' said Henry, and immediately wished he hadn't.

'Dropped in - dropped in!' guffawed the Queen, and Henry held on for dear life as the carriage shook with her laughter. 'Ooh you are a one, and no mistake!'

Suddenly she remembered herself and became solemn again.

'Not in front of the grubs,' she said in a stage whisper, and she tapped again for the carriage to proceed.

Finally they arrived in a warm, cosy little room which could only just accommodate the bulk of the Queen. She clambered heavily down from the carriage and squeezed herself in beside a stout table, laden with food, indicating to Henry the empty seat opposite.

'I haven't dined out for ages,' she said excitedly. 'I am so glad you came> I really was getting just a bit bored, but you know how it is - you never get round to doing anything new until you have guests. Now eat up - you really look as though you could do with a square meal.'

Henry was indeed feeling more than a little hungry again, and his appetite was made keener by the relief at having found himself in such friendly company after the menace that had dogged his footsteps since he re-entered Barraclough House. For some time there was only the sound of contented eating, but eventually, the table was empty and two attendant ants appeared with a flask of honeydew liquor.

Henry contentedly sipped the sweet, cloying liquid and began to tell the Queen of the ants, the reason for his sudden appearance in her presence.

The Queen listened patiently, sipping occasionally from her goblet. Only once did she interrupt him.

'Watch Beetle?' she said 'I knew him as a grub. His dad was a fine fellow, I remember - used to make me laugh, just like you do.'

'You mean you've met the beetles?' Henry was staggered.

'Course I have dearie - though come to think of it it's ever such a long time since I saw any of them around. They seem to have all moved out. Pity really - we used to have such fun in the old days. They're a jolly lot those beetles.'

So then Henry explained about why the beetles had gone away, and the Queen's face became more and more solemn and thoughtful and finally she said.

'Them and their silly soldiers - I've warned them before. Time I sorted them out.' she heaved herself to her feet.

'You mark my words,' she continued grimly. 'Young Denzil will be behind all this - Denzil 942. I' ve always said he was a wrong 'un.'

And a moment ;later the two guards were summoned again and despatched in search of the carriage.

CHAPTER SEVENTEEN

'Parade ground,' snapped the Queen. Henry realised that she was not at all pleased with what she had heard. 'Make it quick!'

The grunts and groans redoubled, and the carriage finally set off at quite a reasonable pace - not enough to ruffle Henry's hair, but fast enough to have the great bulk at his side wobbling perilously. Henry once again clung on to the side of the carriage, trying to avoid being bounced out onto the track.

Suddenly the Queen rapped sharply with her cane on the backs of her straining minions, and the carriage came to an abrupt halt.

'You can wait here,' she said to Henry. 'No need to cause more of a stir than necessary. If you step onto the ledge there, you should get a good view. I'll pick you up later.' and in a moment, the carriage was gone, leaving Henry alone and bemused in the tunnel.

Henry saw a passageway leading off at an angle, and made his way down it towards the smoky light at the far end. He emerged on a ledge, somewhat lower than the one he had first found, but still with a clear view of the encampment below.

Henry held his breath.

The whole army seemed to be on the march. Just below his vantage point, a thousand pairs of feet marched in perfect unison, the beat of their passage thundering through the echoing cavern. A thousand lances glinted in the smoky light of the fires.

There were barked commands, and at each of them, a thousand shining suits of armour swung as one, to march back again, the feet pounding, tramp, tramp, tramp over the dusty floor.

At the far end of the parade ground was a raised dais. As Henry watched, the splendid figure of an ant in full dress armour appeared on the dais.

A thousand marching pairs of feet came to an instant halt. A single command rang out. A thousand glistening swords suddenly whistled about the heads of the warriors in a sighing salute. Then with a resounding crash, the thousand warriors were at sharp attention, each sword sloped precisely to the shoulder, each shining back as straight as a ramrod.

The commander spoke.

'Comrades!' he bellowed, his voice ringing out though the sudden silence of the cavern. 'Our hour has come. Together, we shall drive the last remnants of the enemy from our beloved soil. We shall win a glorious victory, and our deeds will echo down the years....'

A thousand ant voices roared out in a spontaneous cheer, which was instantly silenced by an imperious gesture from the commander.

'Comrades - the battle may be hard fought - but we have the will to win, and the strength to carry our fight into the very heart of the enemy camp. By the rising of the sun, we shall have - VICTORY!'

Once again there was a tumult of cheering, and the wicked swords swished in an arc over the helmeted heads.

Once again the cheering stopped.

This time though, it was from no signal from the resplendent figure on the platform. He stood there, staring in puzzlement, as a thousand armoured warriors before him suddenly looked down at their boots.

'Comrades...' faltered the commander, 'Comrades...' but none of the warriors looked up. Some of the rear ranks had begun to fidget uncomfortably.

'Denzil!'

The commander spun round as though he'd been shot in the back. The last few ranks gave up all pretence and scuttled away across the cavern, their swords dropping to the floor of the parade ground with a soft thud as they ran.

For a long moment, the beribboned commander stood transfixed, staring at the towering, bulbous figure in flowing pink flannelette which had appeared on the dais behind him. Then his legs gave way, and he fell to his knees.

'Mother!' he gasped, his voice hollow with horror.

'Denzil!' said the queen coldly. 'Go to your room at once!'

And as the broken figure slouched off the platform, a thousand swords clattered to the ground behind him, and a thousand anxious figures all tried to beat each other to the far off exit of the emptying parade ground.

How long Henry stood staring at the deserted ground with its untidy piles of discarded weapons, he couldn't say. He was fascinated by the exhibition of sheer power which he had just witnessed. Not since the awful day when he had been caught stealing from the larder, had he seen anything like the wrath of the Queen.

Below him, the fires still smoked sootily, but the menace of the place had evaporated at a word from the Queen. With mounting excitement, Henry began to realise that he had accomplished his mission.

Against impossible odds - he had won.

He was aroused from his reverie by the sound of the carriage pulling up at the far end of the passage which led to his ledge. A moment later, a soldier ant appeared, bowing as it walked and touching its helmet in deference to the boy.

"Scuse me, sir,' it said, a touch of sulkiness in its voice, and just a bit too much emphasis on the 'sir'. 'Your carriage is back for you.'

'Thank you,' said Henry graciously, and he followed the still-bowing figure back to the waiting Queen.

'Climb aboard, Henry,' said the Queen quietly. Henry realised it was the first time she had used his name.

'We've got one or two things to put right around here,' she added grimly.

And together they rumbled behind the puffing and groaning team, up the long ramp of corridors towards the upper levels of Barraclough House.

CHAPTER EIGHTEEN

In the cosy room behind the kitchen range of Barraclough House, two thoughtful figures sat disconsolately, one on either side of the brightly blazing fire. Nearby on the table, lay the remains of their meal, still largely untouched. Neither the Watch Beetle nor the Dumble Dor could summon up any appetite for food under the circumstances.

Finally, the Watch Beetle put into words what both of them had been thinking for the past hour or more.

'I should never have sent him,' he said gloomily, 'After all, he's only a kid. What could I possibly have thought he could do against the ants, when I failed all this time to talk to them myself.'

'You can't blame yourself, old chap,' the Dumble Dor said sympathetically. 'After all - his arrival was predicted. It's all there in the Book of the Scarab.'

The Watch Beetle refused to be comforted.

'Yes, and what does it say in the Book of the Scarab? All that glory talk about a strange Prince from another realm to carry the peoples of beetledom to freedom, with the Sword of the Scarab in his hand. It's twaddle, that's what it is - twaddle.' the Dumble Dor was shocked.

'How can you say that about the sacred book?' he said in hushed tones, as though expecting lightening to strike at any moment in the face if this heresy. 'I mean it's - well sacred.' he finished rather weakly.

'Sacred?' said the Watch Beetle contemptuously. 'Let me tell you something about that sacred book - something which my father once told me after a couple of cups of Honeydew too many, something which I've kept to myself ever since.'

'What do you mean?' the Dumble Dor was agog.

'Well, I was sworn to secrecy, when he realised what he'd said, and so must you be. It would spoil a lot of beetle dreams if it ever got out.'

'Count on me,' said the Dumble Dor firmly. 'I won't breathe a word to anyone.

'Well, that sacred book that the Stag Beetle makes such a fuss about never was handed down from generation to generation at all.'

'So where did it come from?'

'It was Stag's Great Uncle Godfrey. He wrote it one wet summer - just before he went off to spread poetry to the wide world, as he put - mad as a hatter.'

'Godfrey the poet,' whispered the Dumble Dor. 'That explains all those funny rhymes in it.'

'Yes, and we've lived by that book ever since,' the Watch Beetle continued sadly. 'You see, Dumble - Our whole life has been just a sham. All those grand meetings of the Council - all quite unnecessary. They were so wrapped up in it all, that they just let the ants walk in and push us out.'

'So why didn't you say anything? I'm not reproaching you or anything, but you knew all the time...'

'You see, Dumble - it wasn't just that my father had sworn me to secrecy. There's a lot of good advice in that book. Oh - it's dressed up in flowery language, and the Stag can make it sound awfully pompous, but it kept us together, it gave us some common cause. You know what the beetles are like. Without the Book of the

Scarab, they'd have been all over the place.'

'But the boy?' the Dumble Dor was puzzled. 'He came, didn't he?'

'Coincidence - pure coincidence. Naturally, when I saw him, I thought that here was a chance to stir them up a bit, and to get a bit of action. It was too good an opportunity to miss..'

'And we've gone and sent him...'

'Exactly - I allowed myself to get carried away, just like the rest of them. It wasn't that I suddenly *believed* in the Book of the Scarab - I suppose I just wanted it to happen. The boy was an opportunity, someone fresh to try where I'd failed. And now I've gone and done it. We'll never see him again.' and a big, round tear trickled down the Watch Beetle's face, shining brightly in the flickering light of the fire.

'The Dumble Dor leapt to his feet. 'We must go after him,' he said excitedly. 'Come on - I'll go and root out a couple of those old swords we had hanging in the Council chamber.

The Watch Beetle shook his head. 'No - there's no use charging off down there just like that. He's gone beyond the places we know, and we're outnumbered thousands to one. We need to think of some plan...'

The two beetles sat on through the afternoon. No plan was forthcoming, and they became even gloomier as they realised how impossible any chance of rescue must be.

It was well into the evening, and the neglected fire was beginning to burn low, when suddenly the door of the room was thrown unceremoniously open. The two beetles were on their feet in an instant.

'Henry!' shouted the Watch Beetle in joy and disbelief, as he stepped forward to welcome the boy. Then he stopped in his tracks.

Behind Henry, two menacing figures had also stepped through the door. Now at either side of the small figure, there stood a towering soldier ant in shining black armour, their spears held at attention.

'So they caught you,' said the Watch Beetle hollowly, and he staggered back, horrified.

'Release him this instant,' said the Dumble Dor bravely, as he stepped forward, a faintly ridiculous figure, with a poker clutched in his hand.

'It's all right,' said Henry reassuringly. 'You don't need to worry. These are just my escort.'

'Your escort?' the Watch Beetle fought back reviving hope.

'Yes,' explained Henry cheerfully. 'Queenie said it was only right that if I was an ambassador, I should have an escort.' He nudged the embarrassed soldiers, who shuffled a couple of paces into the room, their heads suddenly bowed.

'This is Malcolm 72 and Harold 86,' said Henry, by way of introduction. The soldiers bowed '_Oh and Queenie said to ask if she could come right in because it's getting a bit chilly in the passage.'

The two beetles were open-mouthed. 'Queenie?' they said in an incredulous chorus.

'Yes,' replied Henry excitedly. 'She's come with me to have a chat with you, and to say that it's all a mistake, and to let you know that Denzil 942 is going to have to stay in his room for weeks and weeks, and she had no idea what he was getting up to, and she says its hard being a mum nowadays, when your kids don't do as they're told and...'

'Hold on Henry,' the Watch Beetle interrupted. Why don't you invite Queenie in. We can talk about this much more comfortably over a flask of Honeydew.

Henry turned to the door.

'Queenie!' he called. 'It's all right, you can come in now.'

And to the beetles' amazement there appeared in the doorway, the gigantic figure of the Queen Ant, still draped in the pink flannelette. With some difficulty, she squeezed herself through the narrow opening, and waddled over to the fire.

'Thanks Dearie,' she said to Henry. ' I was fair freezing to death out there. I should have got change before coming on I suppose. These are not the best robes for royalty - still, I got a bit carried away,' and she chuckled hugely.

Then she seemed to notice the Watch Beetle for the first time.

'My!' she exclaimed. 'Haven't you grown.'

CHAPTER NINETEEN

Henry was tired, and just a little sad, as he finally snuggled down under the silken covers of the ceremonial visitors' bed in the guest room of the ant quarters of Barraclough House. It had been agreed that he should spend this night with the ants, who were eager to show that they were quite capable of equalling the hospitality of the beetles.

It had been a day to remember. The Queen had declared it a public holiday, in spite of some mutterings from her worker ants, who had complained that they would get bored. The beetles had responded by making it a national Beetle Festival Day, since it was hard to have a public holiday when none of them really did anything most of the time anyway.

Each tribe had tried to outdo the other in friendly rivalry. The day had begun with a splendid march past of the ant army, only slightly diminished in grandeur by the Queen's refusal to let them have their weapons back. There had been much feverish improvisation before the event, and when the moment had come for them to march, the beetles who had all been given free tickets by the butterflies, were lining the route in eager anticipation.

Finally Denzil 942 appeared. He had been given a day out by the Queen on a pledge of good behaviour, and he was once again to head his magnificent troops. He was resplendent in full dress armour - a brazen helmet with a brilliant white plume bobbing above, a steely breastplate inlaid with mother-of-pearl, and crowned with epaulettes of startling red silk. He marched proudly onto the drill square with a large soup ladle at the slope over his left shoulder.

Denzil barked a command, and the army marched smartly into view, high-kicking in perfect harmony along the square.

'Halt!' bellowed Denzil. 'Displaaay arms!'

'A thousand twigs of Privet swished through the air in a whispering arc. The Queen nudged Henry, who was seated next to her on the dais reserved for the guests of honour.

'He's not a bad lad,' she confided lovingly. 'He's worked ever so hard, you know.'

Henry nodded his agreement.

'Very impressive ma'am,' said the Watch Beetle, who was seated at her other side.

'Ma'am, ma'am?' said the Queen loudly. 'Known him since a grub, and he calls me ma'am. Now you call me Queenie, same as the rest of them>' and she aimed a resounding nudge at his dignified waistcoat. Denzil turned and glared.

'Oops, sorry, Denzil love.' the Queen giggled. 'You can carry on now.'

'Baawt turn!' bellowed Denzil - and a thousand armoured figures turned on their heel.

'Qui-iick march!' - and a thousand pairs of metal-shod boots pounded a harsh rhythm back across the parade ground. A thousand twigs of Privet bobbed at their shoulders.

The beetles cheered until they were hoarse.

Then it was the beetles' turn to entertain.

First half a dozen stick insects came on and did an impression of a tree, which was good for the first five minutes, but went on, Henry felt, just a little bit too long. Still - everyone applauded wildly when the finally disentangled themselves and bowed their way off, though nobody actually shouted 'encore!'.

Then two large Stag Beetles came on for a wrestling bout, which

85

would have been very exciting indeed, except that they got their antlers firmly wedged together at the beginning of the first round, and having defeated everyone's attempts to untangle them, they had to be carried off by a squad of ants, still firmly locked together.

'Will they be all right?' asked Henry anxiously.

'Course they will,' the Dumble Dor was full of contempt. 'Always happens that - bit of nut oil and they'll be as right as nine pence.'

As the afternoon wore on there were all sorts of feats of daring and artistry to divert the happy crowd. Ants and beetles worked together to put on such a show as had never before been witnessed. There were chariot races - each chariot an upturned shell, drawn by an eager team of ants, and driven by an excited beetle.

There was a grand fly-past of Cockchafers, who almost caused a stampede by overshooting the edge of the parade ground and bouncing off the wall of the cavern onto the heads of the audience, like a shower of falling coconuts.

Even the butterflies had been persuaded to perform - a haunting, airborne ballet, full of colour and light, though they rather spoiled it at the end by an unpleasant little argument over payment, which the Watch Beetle promised them they would get at the end of the evening and not before.

'Need them for screen duties tonight,' he explained to Henry in a whisper. 'If I pay them now, they'll go and squander it all on hard nectar, and they'll be fit for nothing this evening.'

All too soon, it seemed to Henry, it was over, and time to dress for dinner and the ball which was to follow.

And what a ball it was.
The food exceeded even the feast which had been Held in Henry's

honour when he had so unexpectedly arrived among them. The ants had made their own contributions, piquant and mysterious. And so much the merrier the whole thing was, because ant sat next to beetle alternately around the long tables, chattering away like long-lost friends.

Then it was time for the dance, and ant and beetle alike took to the floor, high-stepping to the merry sounds of the cricket band. |The hidden corridors of Barraclough House rang that night to the sound of happy laughter, and shone with the lights of a thousand glow-worms. Even the Queen joined in the dancing, her huge abdomen wobbling dangerously across the floor, scattering unwary dancers in all directions.

Eventually, late in the night, Henry had found himself once again, alone in the company of the Watch Beetle and the Dumble Dor. All but the most determined revellers had staggered off to bed, and those who remained sat rather dazedly around, or swayed uncertainly to the slowing music of the cricket band.

'Well Henry,' said the Watch Beetle solemnly. 'Your job seems to be over and done here, and no mistake. You've earned your place in the New History of the Scarab, but I suppose now you really ought to be getting back home.'

Henry though, for the first time in days of the other world of Barraclough House - the world that he really inhabited. He was suddenly overcome with a strange sadness, torn between his new friends here and the family which must surely be worrying about him up there in the world of humans.

'Will I see you again?' he asked, and his voice quavered alarmingly.

'Oh, I expect you will,' answered the beetle. But there was a note of sadness in the voice, and the Dumble Dor was closely studying his boots.

'Well, you must get some sleep now,' the Watch beetle went on, a huskiness in his throat betraying the cheerfulness of his tone. 'We'll sort it all out in the morning.'

The Dumble Dor cleared his throat loudly. 'Good night, Henry,' he said. And impulsively, Henry gave him a big hug, burying his face in the warm mustiness of the woolly waistcoat with its pungent scent.

Then, tearing himself away, he set off resolutely to his room and its silken bed, without glancing back.

On the darkening platform, two dejected figures gazed silently at the retreating boy.

CHAPTER TWENTY

Henry stood nervously looking over the edge of the battlements which crowned Barraclough House. The ground seemed to be miles below him, and all the logic which had seemed so clear when the Watch Beetle was explaining it to him earlier, had now evaporated in the bright afternoon sunshine. Were they really asking him to launch himself off into space, he asked himself. Somehow, up here, the idea had lost any appeal it might have had. He ran through again in his mind, the arguments of the Watch Beetle which had seemed so convincing at the time.

'You see, Henry,' he had explained. 'When you arrived among us, it was because something unusual had happened. After all, everything that's happened to you since we met has been impossible. So what we need to do is to make sure that something unusual happens again. Do you follow?'

'I think so,' Henry said doubtfully. 'But what exactly do I do to make this unusual thing happen?'

'Quite simple really. This morning, you're going to stop doing that falling thing, and you're going to fly - properly I mean. After all, old Dumble here can do it, and that ought to be impossible too, if the truth were told.'

Henry had tried a couple of exploratory flaps of his arms, but he had to admit that he felt not the least bit lighter for it. The Watch Beetle looked amused.

'Not here,' he said. 'What you need is somewhere where you can start with the falling thing, and then change it into flying. Somewhere where you've got plenty of room to get the hang of it. We'll go up to the roof. You can start from there.'

Henry had gasped. 'You surely don't mean for me to jump off the roof?'

'That's right - that way you'll have all the time in the world.'

'But what if it doesn't happen. What if I just fall?' Henry was feeling decidedly unhappy about the turn events were taking.

'That's the beauty of it,' answered the Watch Beetle confidently. 'You see, if you just do your falling thing, then noshing unusual will have happened. You'll simply find yourself back in your bedroom before the start of your adventures, and none of this will have happened.'

'But that will leave you back in the same state you were in before.'

'That's a chance we'll have to take,' the Watch Beetle said generously. 'Now come on. It's a long way up to the roof, and we haven't got all day.'

So Henry had said a last, tearful good-bye to the Dumble Dor, and had followed the Watch Beetle on the long trek up to the rooftop of Barraclough House. Now he was standing, waiting for his courage to join him up here, and it seemed to have got lost, somewhere in the passageways of the upper levels.

'Now remember,' the Watch Beetle said, perched on the parapet beside the frightened boy. 'There's nothing that can go wrong. Either you fly, and it takes you home again, or you don't - and you never left in the first place.'

'Henry turned to him. 'Will I see you again, ' he asked, rather plaintively.

'I won't try to lie to you Henry. I don't know the answer to that one. Let's just decide that you will - after all, it's happened once, so who's to say it won't happen again, the next time we need you.'

Henry was unconvinced. Suddenly he simply didn't want to leave this happy world where he seemed to belong, where he had so many friends, and where nobody ever told him to tidy his room, or made him suit in draughty old churches all day, rubbing away at mouldy old brasses.

'Couldn't I stay a little bit longer,' he asked wistfully.

'I think you've stayed as long as we dare, Henry. There's no knowing how things will turn out if we don't get you home soon. Supposing they missed you?'

'You mean they haven't been out looking for me?' Henry was incredulous.

'No - as far as they're concerned, all this never happened. But you must go. Good-bye Henry.'

And to Henry's chagrin, the Watch Beetle hopped off his perch on the parapet and spiralled away downwards, until he had dwindled to a tiny dot far below. Henry watched until he could see him no more, then gathering his courage, he jumped.

Flying was a strange sensation.

Henry didn't even know how he was doing it, but for a while he was content to revel in his new-found freedom of the air. But although he was undoubtedly flying, yet he was, at the same time, flying ever downwards, and eventually the inevitable happened, and the ground was rushing up to meet him.

Landing was a feeling like the one at the dentists where they put that mask on your face and suddenly everything goes all marsh-mallow with strange whirring and bumping sounds in your ears.

But Henry didn't remember that. What Henry remembered was waking up in the warm sunshine on a mossy bank next to the threadbare lawns.

He looked around him just in time to see a small, very black beetle, scuttling away into the undergrowth.

Someone was calling him to tea. Henry picked himself up and walked slowly and thoughtfully back to Barraclough House.

The End?

Printed in the United Kingdom
by Lightning Source UK Ltd.
110901UKS00001B/82-84